DECLAN'S OMEGAS FATED

Creekside Township Rivals

Book 6

JT Fader

Published by Steambath Press
A Creekside Township Rivals Romance

Paperback published March 2024
ISBN-13: 978-1-998008-52-0

Chapter One | Declan

I leaned back in my chair and stared at the ceiling. Why I had chosen accounting as a profession was becoming less clear by the second. It was tax time and a steady parade of shoeboxes filled with receipts was making its way into my small, cramped office.

The township of Riverton was thrilled to have an accountant in their midst. Some businesses had started coming to me as soon as I set up shop, allowing me time to enter all their information into my accounting software and keep it up to date month by month.

Others—not so much.

Now, it was crunch time. The end of March. I'd be working late nights, sifting through everything so I could produce financial reports that I'd be able to use to file tax returns.

I'd hired an assistant, Carol. A human who knew her way around bookkeeping. She was busy sorting through each business' jumble of papers and ordering them by month and whether they were a sale or an expense. By the time I received the shoeboxes, they were more manageable.

She was a godsend.

I took the lid off an actual file box. Some attempts had been made to keep things orderly in addition to Carol's efforts. Everything was legible and had notes attached to clarify expenses.

There were two boxes in all.

Creekside Motors.

They weren't the first business from Creekside I'd agreed to take on. I lifted a stack of sales slips from what looked to be the repair side of the business. According to my records, they also had a gas station and a convenience store. The latter, I was not looking forward to.

I held the slips to my face and inhaled. There were three distinct scents. Three Omegas. I focused on one strongly enticing my inner wolf. It made my heart beat faster and my cock pulse.

It might mean one thing.

Maybe.

I didn't have time to explore it further even though it pulled at my gut.

I dismissed my reaction and set the papers on my desk. It was going to be difficult to process this business' books with that Omega wolf's scent distracting me. I turned in my chair to face the credenza behind my desk and flicked on the aromatherapy atomizer I used to calm myself.

It *should* cover his scent.

I remained content as I worked for the next 6 hours, flipping through papers, and entering them into the software. The business was well run with a healthy profit margin every quarter.

There were a couple of receipts that needed clarification. I found the *Creekside Motors* phone number in the file I had set up for them on my computer.

Someone picked up after the third ring.

"Hello, Creekside Motors."

My heart raced, replaying the sound of his voice on repeat. Hearing it was like discovering a new song I hadn't known I already knew the rhythm and melody for.

I gripped the phone, my palm sweaty. I hadn't expected to ever find him. I'd spent many years in Metro City, waiting for my fated mate to cross paths with me.

I'd given up hope.

Now here—practically in the middle of nowhere.

I cleared my throat.

"This is Declan from Cooper Accounting. I'm looking for Patrick."

I could hear him breathing, my fated mate, ragged and shallow.

He felt it too—the pull.

"Speaking," he said at last.

Patrick.

My fated mate's name was Patrick.

"I have some questions about a few of your receipts."

"Oh?"

I needed to meet him—and soon.

"Do you mind coming to Riverton? Or I could come to you."

"Can we not discuss it over the phone?"

"I'd prefer if we met." Surely, my voice was enough for Patrick to realize who I was. How this meeting would change our lives. My canines descended and I growled softly.

A gentle whine traveled down the phone line.

"Alpha ... I'm not sure about this."

"Because I'm in Riverton?"

"Because you're the leader of a rival pack."

That hadn't mattered for my brother, Mark. He'd met Reese, fallen in love, and chosen to be with Reese and his little pup, setting aside decades of being the pack leader. They weren't even fated, but my brother had been willing to give up his leadership for Reese.

I had no intention of ever doing that. The Riverton pack was currently in a state of flux. I'd shaken things up when I'd taken over as leader over seven years back, challenging the members to consider new ideas. It was the pack of my birth. I was determined to reform their antiquated ways.

I'd given up a thriving business and a group of amazing friends to come home to do so. I missed my friends. The nights of going out to pubs and those nights when we all stayed in and watched a movie or played board games. Leaving behind the close-knit group had been the hardest thing I'd ever done, but I'd decided that my pack needed to come first.

Regardless, I could put my pack first *and* pursue my fated mate.

"I'm not sure that's going to stop us," I said.

A cheeky response—but the truth.

Another whine through the phone line. "I can't leave for another hour."

"I'll be waiting for you." I smiled as Patrick groaned. "Meet me at my office."

The call ended abruptly. I'd overwhelmed him. I'd need to make it up to him. I lifted a clipped stack of his receipts and ran my nose across them, picking up the details of his scent.

I growled as I sniffed the slips of paper.

I was interrupted by a knock on my door. Carol poked her head in.

"I'm going to head out, Declan. Have you got enough to keep you busy?"

"I'll be here until late. Thank you." Not doing anyone's books, though. It wouldn't be long until my fated mate arrived in my office. I was surprised I hadn't detected the significance of his scent sooner. Even more surprised that I'd tried to ignore it.

"Who brought in the *Creekside Motors* stuff?"

"One of the two partners. Tyler, I think."

I had caught the second scent on the outside of the box as well as Patrick's. It had a pleasant appeal to it. The third scent was only on some of the sales and expense sheets.

The file boxes were mainly permeated by the *Creekside Motors* partners' scents.

They complimented each other.

"Thank you, Carol. Have a good night."

Carol nodded. "Try to get some sleep at some point." Then she left me alone. I looked around the room. It was a mess of papers and file folders stacked on various pieces of furniture.

I would need to clear some of it to make room.

Patrick and I wouldn't be doing much talking.

I lifted my neat piles of documents off the sofa, moved them to the credenza, and retook my place behind my desk to pass the rest of the time.

I couldn't concentrate. I was nervous. I'd spent the last 10 years rutting my way through the Omega population, male and female, in the city. The encounters had never meant anything before.

I'd come close to matching myself with a chosen mate a couple of times, but the relationships had always felt devoid of what I craved. I'd decided to remain unmatched instead.

It would be different with Patrick. I didn't want to mess it up. I busied myself entering the easiest documents from the convenience store. All the packing slips for their inventory.

I lifted my head from what I was doing.

Patrick's scent overwhelmed my senses before he even entered through the front door. I rose from my desk, preparing myself for the first sight of him. I hadn't expected him so soon. He must have left immediately after my call and rushed to Riverton in less than an hour.

I went to my office door and opened it. Standing in the middle of the reception area—the most gorgeous and seductive-looking wolf I had ever set eyes on. He was stunning. Thick, dark blond hair cut short on the sides, and pale blue eyes filled with unbridled desire peering at me. His face was ruddy from exposure to the spring cold, explaining the black leather jacket and chaps.

He had sped here on his motorcycle.

He made the first move, launching himself at me. His gloved hands gripped my face, and his lips came crashing down on mine. I spun him and shoved him against the wall, pinning him to its wood-paneled surface as I deepened the kiss, running my tongue past his lips.

His mouth tasted like heaven.

Patrick's arms collided with my chest as he unzipped his coat. I had to release him so he could remove it and his gloves. My white buttoned shirt was next to be discarded.

It soon landed in a pile next to his coat on the floor.

I'd never felt this desperate before. Patrick's scent and taste were taking me in unprecedented directions. My entire world was colored by his presence. I wanted to climb inside him.

Make him mine.

I hauled him into my office and pressed the door closed in case Carol decided to come back for some reason. As far as she knew, I wasn't seeing anyone.

She wouldn't understand the lust-driven attraction between fated mates. I made short work of Patrick's tight black t-shirt, dragging it up and over his head.

Our lips met again, frantic, and desperate. Patrick moaned into my mouth as I thumbed his nipple. I cruised further down, teasing the sensitive skin of his abs. They jumped and clenched beneath my fingers. I brushed my palm across the hard muscles, wondering what they would feel like beneath my curious warm lips. I sank to my knees to find out.

It took me a second to figure out how to remove his leather chaps. He had to help me, releasing the buckles near his waist. They fell to the floor at his feet. I clung to his hips as I kissed his belly.

I took a moment to look up at him from my position kneeling at his feet.

The word *Adonis* formed in my mind.

He was beautiful.

I had to *pull* my attention away. Patrick ran his hand through my hair as I breathed in his scent and ran my lips back and forth over his abs. On top of his body's natural essence, I could detect the odor of vehicle oil and gasoline. And a strong overtone of his business partner's scent.

I kissed his jeans fly. My fated mate groaned, and his cock hardened beneath my touch. My fingers fumbled to release him. I peeled his jeans and underwear away, revealing his cock.

It was perfection—long and thick.

I pressed it against his stomach and ran my tongue along its silky length.

Stopped. And looked up at him.

His cock smelled and tasted of his business partner.

Patrick touched my cheek. "I'll explain later, Alpha."

I rose to my feet and cupped his face in both hands. "You're my fated mate. I accept you've sought pleasure elsewhere." To emphasize my words, I kissed him. He was mine, but I'd be delusional to expect that he didn't already have a life that included rutting with someone else.

Patrick shifted his weight back and forth, removing his pants as he clung to my shoulders after shoving his jeans off his hips. I took a step back to admire him while dispensing of my dress pants.

My cock throbbed at the full sight of him. I stepped over to the sofa, sat on it, and patted my left thigh. I wanted his back to my chest so he could feel my rapid heartbeat against his spine.

He followed my direction, seating himself facing away from me. I grabbed his chin and turned his face so our lips could explore the intricacies of our shared desire again.

He moaned and deepened our kiss, assaulting my mouth, as I stroked his cock. He spread his legs to give me better access and shifted, his ass cheeks hanging off my leg and between my thighs.

I moved my hand from his cock to his balls, caressing them. Then tickled his taint.

He mewled into my mouth, then pulled away from it.

"Please, Alpha," he whined. "Alpha, please touch me."

I'd never encountered anyone so needy. Whining, panting, and rocking his hips to try and move my hand to other places. I lifted my hand away and fed Patrick's mouth my finger.

He melted against my chest as he sucked and coated it in saliva.

Patrick begged again as I circled his hole with my wet finger. It pulsed beneath my touch. His body was aching for me. I pressed my finger inside him. He pushed down on it, taking me in further. He tipped his head back on my shoulder, reached up, and gripped the back of my neck.

He mewled sweetly and clawed at me every time I plunged my finger into him.

One—then two after I spat on my fingers.

I held him tight against me, my arm across his chest, my fingers under his arm. He lifted his arm above his head. I ran my nose through the coarse blond hair under his arm. His scent there was sweaty and salty. I ran my tongue over the area and became instantaneously addicted.

I played with his nipple while I nuzzled, licked, and inhaled his pure maleness.

I ran my hand from his nipple, down his chest, to his abs. I clung to them as they clenched and released as he rode my fingers. He whimpered when I removed the penetration.

My cock was hard and aching beneath his ass cheek, my precum painting his skin. I lifted his ass, adjusted my position, and pressed my cockhead to his hole.

When I thrust it home past his loosened ring, Patrick cried out with the most incredible sound. Half howling—half cursing. He was the one to sit forward and sink completely on me.

I placed my hands on his hips and encouraged him to rise and fall. Each time he impaled himself on me, he grunted, moaned, and called out, "Yes, Alpha."

I spat into my hand and grabbed his cock, stroking him. His channel pulsed around me. His voice grew louder. A glorious sound filled the room as he roared and spilled his seed on my hand.

I pumped my hips harder and faster against him. He held steady, leaning back on one hand, taking me all the way in. His body fit perfectly with mine. I hammered into him.

A howl built in my chest and erupted from my throat as I filled my fated mate with my seed. If they were working late, there was no way the neighboring offices hadn't heard us.

I didn't care.

My fated mate had come to me.

Now, what was the deal with his business partner?

Chapter Two | Patrick

Declan had his back against the leather sofa cushions with me wrapped in his arms. I cozied in not sure what had come over me. I knew the attraction to your fated mate was meant to be incredible.

It had taken me by surprise.

I wasn't sure how Logan had resisted Harlan for so long.

I must be weak. It felt like my longing for Declan came from my bones. I looked up at him. He was watching me. I smirked at him.

"Hi, I'm Patrick."

Declan's chest shook as he laughed. "I'm Declan. Pleasure to meet you."

I stroked his face. "That's for sure."

He kissed the surface of my palm; the affectionate touch gave me shivers of pleasure. We needed to clarify something. It was obvious Declan had detected Tyler on my skin.

"I've never rutted with him," I said.

"We're talking about your business partner?"

"We've been friends for over twenty years."

"And that's the reason he had your cock in his mouth today?"

"We have an arrangement."

"Some arrangement."

I turned in his arms so I could see his face better. "Look … not going to lie. Tyler and I are close. We've been through a lot together. But we're not *together*."

"It's never come up?"

"What? Being a mated pair? We're two Omegas."

"Would that really matter? I've heard Carl is a liberal leader."

Of course, it had crossed my mind. I loved Tyler. Like truly loved him. But it was one-sided. He'd made it very clear that what we had was simply two Omega best friends seeking comfort.

Even six years ago when he'd had the triplets for Harlan and Logan, Tyler had barely tolerated my increased attention. At least that's what it had felt like. I'd initiated every affectionate touch.

My arm around his shoulders. Holding his hand. Kissing his cheek or the side of his head.

All me.

After Tyler whelped the pups, our physical contact had gone back to the way we'd been carrying on for years. It had crushed me not being able to touch him anymore.

I had wanted more from him than kneeling in front of each other when we were horny.

Had wanted.

I'd given up dreaming of a different life for us.

Hearing Declan's voice through the phone had taken a huge weight off my chest. I'd spent too many nights watching Tyler sleep in the bed next to mine.

Staring at his lips.

Wishing I could kiss them.

I played with the hair on Declan's chest. He was my fated mate but my primal longing was still stronger for Tyler. It didn't make any sense.

"Are you all right?" Declan asked. "You seem deep in thought."

"The urge to mate with you was stronger than I ever could have imagined." I smiled at Declan and dismissed Tyler from my mind. I rolled away from him and looked at the room.

"Looks like an organized bomb went off in here," I said.

"I'm up to my eyeballs in business receipts." Declan ran his fingers through my hair. "Your intoxicating scent on your paperwork was very distracting this afternoon."

I bit my bottom lip, turned in his arms, and took a moment to gaze into his eyes. They were warm and brown like his hair. Earthy. They made me feel protected. Such an Omega thing.

Couldn't stop it.

I really was weak.

"And now?" I asked.

Declan growled and chased my mouth for a kiss. After he had caressed every surface past my lips, he left me with a kiss on the tip of my nose. "Your scent makes me want to eat you."

"I sense that might have to wait."

Declan sighed and looked over my shoulder at his desk. "I can't take the 10 days to mate with you. It's tax season. I won't be able to take that much time off."

My heart felt like it sank into my stomach. I wanted to spend the next 10 days and nights locked in his arms being drilled into some bedding and filled until I was dripping with his seed.

I wanted what Tyler had experienced. An opportunity to have pups.

On the rare occasions when we had talked about our lives, neither of us had predicted we would ever have pups. Some delusional part of my brain had told me it was because Tyler and I were meant to be together as a mated pair. Reading the room, though … I knew not to suggest it.

"How long can you give me?" I asked.

"I can come to see you a few times this week. Spend the night." I looked down at his chest. He raised my face using one finger under my chin. "What are you not telling me?"

"Tyler and I are roommates." That wasn't the full story. "We share a bedroom."

Declan furrowed his brow. "The same bed?"

I shook my head. "No, nothing like that." Except when he was pregnant. Sometimes I ended up on his bed rubbing his back until he fell asleep. I would often pass out behind him.

I may have kissed the back of his head a few times.

I had.

My heart had thundered in my ears as I'd set my lips against his hair, part of me wanting him to still be awake. All of me wanting him to roll over to face me and take my mouth with his.

We'd never kissed. It was a massive regret that we hadn't incorporated that level of intimacy into our encounters. Just a quick make-out session before going down on each other.

That might have satisfied me.

I brushed my hand up Declan's jawline and kissed him.

Here I was with my fated mate ... and I wished I was kissing Tyler.

"Do you mind driving out to my place?" Declan asked.

"I can make it work. You're only an hour away. I can spend my nights with you."

Declan smiled at me; the excitement reached his eyes. "Yeah?"

"You'll have to promise me you won't work too late."

"Mm." He touched my bottom lip. "I'm all yours after 8. Is that all right?"

I caught his finger with my teeth, sucked the tip, and released it. "Perfect."

"What about tonight?"

I groaned. I wanted to stay with him, but we had the pups for a sleepover tonight. All four of them. Haley, Rose, Harry, and Reese Jr. We had promised to watch them so Harlan and Logan could have some private time together. At the age of five, they had all shifted out of wolf form.

Now at the age of six, they were a handful, but Tyler and I spent a lot of time with them. We saw them at least twice a week. The pups called Tyler *Papa Tyler*. I was Uncle Patrick.

I saw so much of Tyler in Rose and Harry; it sometimes made my heart hurt a little.

That I hadn't given him those pups.

"I can't tonight. We're watching four six-year-old pups overnight for some friends."

"Four?"

"Long story." I sat up. "It'll take both Tyler and me to wrangle them."

"Sounds like a sleepless night."

I rose from the sofa and set my attention on finding my clothes. "We'll wear them out. We're used to watching them. We have a few tricks."

"The sire and carrier … they're good friends of yours?" Declan joined me in redressing.

"We have a strong connection." I wasn't going to get into what that connection was. Declan and I needed to spend more time getting to know each other before I told him about Tyler's life.

"Are you sure you can't sit it out?"

"No, it wouldn't be fair to Tyler."

I crossed the room and slung my arms around Declan's neck. Driving away from him was going to be difficult. My hormones wanted to spend the next 10 days and nights with him.

So far, I was enamored with him. He seemed understanding. Recognized I had a life apart from him that was important to me. I had stood my ground. Maybe I wasn't so weak after all.

We clung tightly to each other as we kissed. The contact filled a deep need in me I had never experienced before when kissing someone. Not that my experience was broad. I'd had moments with a few Alphas over the years. Some had expressed wanting to make me their chosen mate.

My love for Tyler had always stopped me.

Declan smiled against my lips, then held my face, and stared into my eyes.

"I'm looking forward to talking to you. Finding out everything about you."

That sentiment made my heart soar. I wanted to know my fated mate before we had a pup on the way. We weren't from the same pack. I knew very little about him. I'd heard he was a good leader, trying to reform his pack to be more like East Creekside. That's all I knew.

And that he was an accountant.

I smiled at him. "Not much to tell. I might bore you."

Declan shook with laughter. "Never. I plan on giving you my every attention." He lowered his hands and encircled my shoulders. I stepped closer into his arms to revel in the hug. He was quite a bit taller than me. Tall enough that he could kiss the top of my head.

I was lucky.

My fated mate had a sweet side and had promised to shower me with it.

I had been right. It was hard to pull away from him, walk out the door, and fire up my motorcycle. Every mile I put between us gave me a sick feeling in my stomach.

I longed to be back in his arms.

When I pulled up outside our house, Tyler was in the front field chasing four running and screaming little creatures. The sight of them enjoying themselves brought me out of my funk.

I parked the bike, stripped out of my motorcycle gear, and joined them.

Rose flew at me and launched herself into my arms. "Uncle Patrick, you're home!" She wrapped her chubby little arms around my neck and kissed my cheek.

This … this here. This was home. With Tyler and the four young wolves. My desire for Declan faded into the background as I turned my attention toward my family.

I set Rose down on the ground and tucked her unruly blond curls behind one ear. She was a wild one. So was Harry. The two who reminded me so much of Tyler. The other two were all Harlan. Haley and Reese Jr took after their sire. Dark features and serious natures. But even they were enjoying the game of chase. Tyler ran toward me, panting.

"So glad you're home," he said. "They're wearing me out." He pounded me on the shoulder. "So … tell me. Was he your fated? This Declan?"

I nodded. "Absolutely. Barely said two words to each other until after."

Tyler grinned at me. "So excited for you, bro. You found your fated mate."

I hated it when he called me *bro*. It reminded me that aside from the blowjobs, that's all we were. Really good friends. Like brothers. Now all of that was going to change.

"He seems nice enough," I said, trying to find anything at all to add.

"So why are you back here? Shouldn't you be mating with him?"

"It's tax season. He can't take the time off."

Tyler crossed his arms. "Oh. That's got to be rough."

"I'll be fine. I'm seeing him tomorrow night."

Tyler shoved me. "Was the mating good?"

I smirked. "He's very commanding. Warmed me up in all the right places."

"Nice."

We were torn from our conversation by the sound of Haley screaming. It appeared that Harry had run into her and knocked her over. Apparently, it was a life-threatening injury.

Tyler was the first to arrive and scoop her up.

"I think we should head in for a bedtime snack," I suggested. It was past 6. The light was fading, and it was time to wind them down for the night.

The other three followed us as Tyler carried Haley up the stairs and into the house. Luckily, it was quiet. The rest of the house knew we were having the pups over for a sleepover. They'd do their best to stay quiet. Likely, a lot of watching television in their rooms.

We set a bowl of blueberries in front of each of them. Reese Jr. nearly nodded off at the table. His eyes kept closing and then he'd jerk awake and start eating again.

Tyler and I grinned at each other, trying not to laugh.

In everything we did with the pups, we always included Reese Jr. We didn't want him to think he was any different than his three siblings. We loved all four of them deeply.

After they finished eating, we ushered them up the stairs. A bathroom break and brushing teeth was next. Then nightgowns and pajamas. We put Haley and Rose in one bed in our room and Harry and Reese Jr. in another, leaving only one bed. When they were still in wolf form, we were able to have them sleep at the end of our beds at our feet. Now, one of us had to take the sofa.

We took turns reading them a short story. Haley passed out before we finished.

Each little wolf received a kiss on the head from both of us and then we snuck out of the room. Tyler closed the door softly and we made our way back downstairs.

I think we were both exhausted when we plopped down on the sofa. It surprised me when Tyler leaned against me and put his head on my shoulder.

"I guess you're not going to be around much longer," he said.

I hadn't thought that far ahead. It made sense that I would go to live with my Alpha. What would that mean for our business ... and our friendship? For our family?

I sucked in a breath as tears formed in my eyes.

I didn't want to leave all of this behind.

"I'm not sure," I answered.

Tyler lifted his head and stared at me. "What? You have to go to your Alpha."

I shrugged. "Do I?"

"Of course you do. You'll have a whole life with him. Have pups. Fall in love."

I looked at Tyler. "I already have all of those things."

Tyler wrinkled his brow. His eyes looked sad. "Patrick, please don't say it."

What?

I bolted up from my seat, crossed the room, and spun back to face him. "You know?"

"Of course, I know. You're my best friend."

"What the hell, Tyler?"

Tyler slumped against the back cushions and folded his arms across his stomach. "I don't want to talk about it. You've found your fated mate. That's all that matters."

Not that easy.

I returned to the sofa and sat beside Tyler. He pulled away from me, creating more distance between us. "So much more than that matters right now. I don't love Declan."

"Yet."

"I know. He's my fated mate. I'll love him in time. But right now, I'm already in love."

Tyler covered his ears. "Please, don't, Patrick. Please … don't."

I could hear my rapid pulse in my ears, thumping. I felt queasy, but it wouldn't be like I was telling him anything he didn't already know. The words were slow to form on my lips.

They came out in a whisper.

"I love you, Tyler."

Tyler burst away from me to the other side of the room. "I told you not to say it."

I jumped up and joined him. "It was time."

"Shitty timing. You've just met your fated mate."

I tried to grab Tyler's arm, but he pulled away. "I don't want to go to Declan without you knowing how I feel about you."

"Why? So, I can suffer?"

This time I managed to secure him by gripping both of his shoulders. The words he'd spoken didn't make sense. "Why would you suffer, Tyler?"

Tyler knocked my hands away. "Can we stop now? Please?"

I held the back of his neck and refused to break eye contact with him. I needed to know what he meant. "Not until you tell me what the hell you're talking about."

It was as if Tyler suddenly deflated. He slumped his shoulders and let his head fall forward until our foreheads were pressed together.

"I love our life together," he said.

"So do I … I don't think I can give it up."

"Fuck," Tyler whispered and clung to the back of my neck. He lifted his chin. I felt his breath mingling with mine. It was a perfect moment. To be followed by another.

Tyler whimpered as he set his lips gently on mine.

My entire world changed. I cupped Tyler's face and returned the soft caress with my lips. A stream of tears ran up against my thumb, trickled around it, and made its way to my wrist.

We ended the kiss. Tyler, in his own way, had told me he loved me too.

Chapter Three | Tyler

God, I loved him. So much. But I had hoped and dreamed Patrick would find his fated mate someday. I didn't want to take that away from him. He deserved every happiness.

Now, we'd messed it all up.

His tears ran onto my lips as we kissed again. Surge and retreat, so unsure of what we were doing. What it meant for us. If it could mean anything at all. We were deep in our love.

I wanted to wrap my heart around him.

I stopped, separated our lips, sniffing as more tears fell, placed my hand on his chest, and pushed him away. "We need to stop." He wouldn't release me. His hand still cupped my face. I turned my head to break contact with him. I could feel my heart shattering.

"I don't think I can do that," Patrick said.

"You've found your fated mate."

"I barely know him."

"You're destined, Patrick. You won't be able to resist him now that you've met him."

Patrick crossed his arms. "Whose idea was it for him to do our taxes?"

"We couldn't have known."

A little voice came from the top of the stairs. It was Rose. "I'm thirsty."

"Well, come down." I motioned for her to follow me into the kitchen. I ran her a tiny amount of water. We didn't need a panicked middle-of-the-night bathroom trip.

I emerged from the kitchen, holding Rose's tiny hand.

"Let's get you back to bed," I said to her.

Rose pointed at Patrick. "Uncle Patrick too."

I looked at him. It was his turn to sleep on the sofa. I was ready to turn in as soon as I had Rose settled. The evening had worn me out. Too may emotions had been revealed.

We'd kissed.

I could still taste him on my lips.

Tomorrow, we could pretend it never happened. Patrick could go to Declan, and they could start their life together. What we had shared would become a distant memory.

A moment of weakness.

Not real life.

Instead of staying behind, Patrick followed me and Rose up the stairs. He took his turn kissing her cheek good night, then stood looking at me.

"I need to lie down," I said.

He sat on the edge of my bed, swung his legs onto it, and lay down. He extended one arm along the edge of my pillow as he set his head on it.

His gaze held mine.

God, I loved him.

I couldn't resist him. I could have turned away and gone back downstairs to sleep on the sofa. Instead, I climbed onto the bed and into his arms. He tugged me until my back was pressed to his chest. He moved his hand from my hip to my chest—and kissed the back of my head.

"I love you," he whispered.

My body shuddered and a new assault of tears was torn from me by the ridiculous situation we were in. "You can't, Patrick. You just can't."

He hugged me closer. His breath was warm on my neck.

"Please let me love you," he said.

"But Declan."

"I won't go to him. I'll stay here with you."

It's what I wanted—to have Patrick stay with me. But I also wanted him to have his fated life. I watched the rise and fall of little Harry's chest. We'd created a life for ourselves without Alphas.

"I love you too." The words had surged up from my chest, starting in my toes. It might be the last time I'd get to say them. There was no stopping a pair of fated mates.

"But I want you to go to him," I added, practically ripping out my own heart. My days and nights were about to get a whole lot darker. So much time had passed, I hadn't thought I'd ever lose him. Even if we'd never become intimate, I would have cherished him forever.

My soul was buried deep within his.

"My family is here," Patrick said. "You and the pups are my family."

"That won't ever change."

"Then why are you pushing me away?"

I rolled to face him and placed my hand on his face. "Because you have the opportunity to experience something few wolves do. A fated mate, Patrick. Please grab onto that."

"I'll never stop loving you."

"You don't have to. I just need you to give Declan a chance."

Patrick sighed. "I'm going to stay on with *Creekside Motors*. I need to see you every day."

I nearly groaned with anguish. Seeing Patrick daily at work, knowing he belonged to another would be torturous, but I couldn't deny him. I knew I would need to see him too.

I rolled back over, my back to his chest. Any longer facing him and I would have kissed him again. I tucked my knees up, fetal. Patrick's knees scooped up behind me.

It felt incredible to be in his arms, cuddled together.

I awoke to someone touching my nose. I blinked, sunlight streaming through the curtains. Rose's precious face was looking at me. A weight on my arm held me in place.

Patrick.

We'd fallen asleep together.

"Were you sleeping?" Rose whispered.

I smiled at her. "I was … but someone tickled my nose."

Patrick shifted behind me. He used my hip to push himself up to see over my shoulder.

"Good morning, Rosie," he said.

"Harry and Reese are hungry," she replied.

I yawned. "Aren't they always."

The mattress bounced as Patrick moved away from me. He patted me on the shoulder. "I'll get them something to eat. You sleep. It's early."

"Nope. I'm awake now." I clambered off the bed and followed Patrick and Rose downstairs. As expected, Harry and Reese had the fridge open and were rooting around in it.

"Get out of there," I said to them.

"Over to the table," Patrick added. "We'll make something."

"Eggs," Harry said.

"Sounds good to me," I replied. Patrick and I bumped into each other as we both reached for the carton of eggs. He set his hand on mine as I grabbed the carton—and lingered.

"Patrick, don't," I whispered and pulled the eggs from the fridge. He sighed, went to the cupboard, and lifted down six glasses. I cracked one egg each in four of the glasses and brought them over to the table. When I returned, Patrick had cracked three eggs each in our glasses.

"Thank you."

Patrick's gaze locked on mine as we both swallowed our eggs. He took my glass from me and set both in the sink. He moved his hand from his glass to my hip—ever so softly.

I trembled at his touch.

"I love you," he mouthed to me.

"Please stop saying that." I removed his hand from my hip and walked over to the kitchen table to make sure all the eggs had been eaten. Haley was poised over her glass, making a game of sucking the yolk in and out of her mouth. "Swallow, Haley."

She dropped the yolk out of her mouth and into her glass. I was stunned it hadn't broken in her mouth yet. "Uncle Jonas lets us have quail's eggs. I like the crunch."

"Uncle Jonas has access to food at cost," Patrick replied. "We're not so lucky. Now eat."

"I hate chicken," Harry piped up.

"Which is why we don't feed them to you," I said.

"I don't like chicken either," Patrick added.

"Won't be long until you can hunt your own game, Harry." I cleared the glasses off the table. Haley had finally swallowed her egg. Another 10 years and they'd all be able to shift back and forth. There would be a celebratory hunt where they'd be taught some hunting skills.

I wondered if Patrick would be around for it.

I turned back from the sink. Patrick was stroking Rose's hair. He would never miss something that monumental. He loved these four small wolves like they were his own.

His loving attention toward them made my insides ache.

We truly had become a family.

And now we'd professed our love for one another.

I had a moment of weakness.

I wandered over to Patrick, wrapped my arms around his waist from behind, and lay my cheek on his back. He leaned back into my embrace and placed his hands on mine.

I kissed the center of his back.

Our charges didn't even notice our closeness. They jumped up, shoved past us, and took off for the front door. They'd want to play outside before we returned them to their home.

"Duty calls," Patrick said and turned in my arms. I kept them in place around his waist. He stroked my jawline in both hands, then cupped my face. "You're so beautiful."

My heart leaped in my chest and thudded a strong erratic pulse through my veins. I was overwhelmed. Patrick was turning my heart inside out. I'd never been so conflicted.

Patrick lowered his lips onto mine. This time I was ready. I raked my hands into his hair and took everything my heart and body needed from him. We both groaned as we separated.

"We should get outside before someone gets hurt," Patrick said.

I licked my lips and nodded my head.

Reluctantly, I headed for the front door. Outside, the little wolves were going wild. Not sure if they were playing chase or tackle. It was only a matter of time until someone was crying.

We herded them toward the playground and took our places encouraging them through the jungle gym of ramps, ropes, slides, and swings. Our eyes locked onto each other's from the opposite sides of the wooden bridge. Patrick smiled at me. The simple gesture made me blush.

God, I loved him.

It was approaching a reasonable time to return the wolves to their protectors. Harlan and Logan would have had enough time to sleep in. It was always bittersweet dropping them at home. It was a relief because they wore us out, but we loved spending time with them.

I loaded them into my truck.

"I'm going to head to the shop," Patrick said as he clung to my baby finger.

"It's Sunday." I tugged on his shirt. "I thought we could spend some time together." He was going to leave me for Declan soon. I wanted every single moment in his arms before that happened.

"I think it's best if I'm not here when you get back."

A flood of tears created a sheen across my eyes, but I nodded in agreement. I motioned over my shoulder. "I should get these ruffians home." I tried to smile at him.

It was a weak effort. Tears ran onto my lips.

"I'm never going to stop loving you," Patrick said.

I sucked in a ragged breath. "Go to your fated mate. Find new love."

Patrick clutched my shirt. "Tyler … I don't want …."

I dragged his hand away from my shirt. "Please, Patrick … go."

Patrick stared at me; his lips pulled between his teeth. He blinked at me a few times, stroked the back of his fingers down my cheek, and turned away from me.

I watched him walk slowly to his truck, climb in, and start it up. He wiped some tears off his face as he drove past me and down the driveway.

My heart shattered for real this time.

Chapter Four | Declan

I hung up the phone. It had made my heart soar, hearing his voice again. Patrick was putting in some extra work at his garage then we would head to my house. He'd called to ask if he could arrive closer to 6 and hang around to wait for me to come home from work.

Maybe prepare something for us to eat.

I needed to connect with my Beta and let her know to expect Patrick—my fated mate. I'd picked up some wine on the way home last night. I wanted tonight to be special.

I was glad there was some fresh venison in the fridge. It would pair nicely with the red wine I had chosen. I had almost phoned Patrick to find out if he had a favorite winery.

The fact he was minding a handful of young wolves had stopped me. He had his hands full. I wanted to spoil him tonight. Help him relax. Mind and body. Spend most of the night talking.

My cock thickened. I also craved the sight, feel, and scent of his body. I would have to fight the desire to mate with my Omega as soon as I walked in the door.

I was surprised I made it until 8 in the evening. A testament to how busy I was with work. It only took me ten minutes to drive home. A shiny restored pickup truck was parked out front.

All the main floor lights were on, creating a warm glow on the front porch.

It felt good. Coming home to someone.

An unusual scent met me as I opened the front door and entered my house. The air was heavy with it. The sounds of something cooking came from the kitchen.

I was intrigued.

In the kitchen, I found my fated mate, my Patrick, standing over the stove with a metal pan I didn't recognize, and holding a fork. He was poking at something sizzling.

He looked up at me and an incredible smile lit up his face.

"Thought I'd surprise you," he said.

I stepped closer to him and put my arm around his shoulders. "I'm surprised. What is it?"

"My friend Jonas introduced me to it. It's bacon. He owns the restaurant *Growlers* in Creekside. They pair it with eggs and put it on stacks of ground meat and bread."

"It's cooked."

Patrick bumped my hip playfully with his. "It's *so* good."

"It smells good, that's for sure."

"I've cut up some venison to go with it." He looked over his shoulder. "Can you open that wine? This is almost ready. It has to be crispy but not black."

"My human friends used to rave about bacon."

"You had human friends?"

"In the city, wolves and humans form close friendships."

"I used to have a few humans I was able to tolerate in high school."

"Are you still friends with them?"

"No, they all moved away … to Metro City."

Patrick lifted the bacon out of its grease, set them on a paper towel, and blotted the strips. I was trusting Patrick that the cooked meat wouldn't upset my stomach. He plated our dinner and followed me into the dining room where I arranged two glasses and the open bottle of wine.

Patrick poured us both a glass, leaned back in his chair, and sipped on it as I saw red and tore into my venison while he waited for his turn.

I grunted at him to go ahead after I finished my meat and looked at the bacon on my plate. I lifted a piece and used my front teeth to tear away a small piece.

It wasn't terrible.

Salty.

Patrick started with his bacon. He hummed as he ate it. It made me smile. He was showing signs of being content in my presence. We could build on that.

I reached for his hand. He bit his bottom lip as he gazed at me and then took my hand in his. I squeezed it, then released him to finish his meal. My Omega was a hearty feeder.

He would bear strong pups.

After we cleaned our faces and hands, I took the wine bottle and my glass and led Patrick to the living room. I topped up his glass and settled in beside him on the sofa.

"Tell me everything about you," I started.

Patrick laughed. "Rather broad. Where would you like me to start?"

"Let's start with your daily life. When did you decide you wanted to be a mechanic?"

"My sire was a mechanic. I started going into the garage with him from the time I was ten. He used to show me a few things. Let me help with small jobs."

"You enjoy it?"

"It brings me a lot of satisfaction."

"And *Creekside Motors* is yours?"

"My sire left it to me, but Tyler and I both run it." A fleeting look of sadness skittered across Patrick's face—then it was gone. Maybe they'd disagreed about something recently.

"You've always lived in Creekside?"

"Whelped there."

"Riverton is my home pack. I left to go to university. Fell in love with Metro City. Decided to stay and set up my business there."

"Then why did you come back?"

"My brother, Mark, called me. Told me he was stepping down as leader."

"I know Mark quite well. Sometimes our young wolves play with their Peter and Mark Jr. I admire him greatly. He's a kind and gentle wolf who loves his family."

I smiled. "And soft. The pack was running all over him. They didn't have solid direction."

"And you decided you could manage them?"

"At first I wasn't sure. I just knew there was no one qualified to take over."

"You kept up with your pack politics?"

"Habit." I studied Patrick as he took a sip of his wine. He had referred to his friends' pups as *our* pups. I wasn't sure what it meant. "You're very close to those four pups."

"We've helped in caring for them since they were whelped."

I waited, but he wasn't offering any more information. I decided to move on. He would let me into his life more when he was ready. Tonight, we'd keep things light.

"What made you want to go into accounting?"

"That is a question I ask myself every day." I refilled my wine glass. I was glad I'd bought more than one bottle. "Seemed like a good idea at the time? That's about all I can offer you."

"You don't enjoy it?"

"No, I do. I like order. It satisfies that need."

Patrick chewed on his bottom lip and then smirked at me. "I have another much more interesting need I'd like to have satisfied right about now."

Cheeky.

Love it.

I set my wine glass down. "Bedroom?"

"I'd prefer that to the sofa. Yesterday was fun but I think we need more space."

"You like to spread out?"

"Planning on spreading all sorts of things for you tonight."

I growled, scooped him up in my arms, and carried him to the bedroom, wine glass and all. He hung backward to place it on the bedside table before I tossed him onto the mattress.

He bounced, making me smile.

Patrick wrapped his arms around my neck as I met him on the bed, layered myself on him, and let the weight of my body press him into the bedding.

I grabbed his hands, stretched his arms up over his head, and pinned them there.

My Omega mewled and sighed and squirmed beneath me.

"Make me yours, Alpha," he whispered, his voice sweet and seductive. I needed to capture any more delectable sounds that came from him. I sealed his mouth with mine.

He moaned and struggled beneath my grip on his arms. I held them fast as I tasted every surface of his lips and tongue. Patrick rocked his hips up, jamming his hard cock against mine.

I released his arms, but he kept them draped over his head. I pulled my lips away from his. He tipped his chin up, chasing them, wanting them back. He whined when I denied him of them.

I kissed him from the tip of his chin, along his jawline, to behind his ear. Then lower, sucking and licking his neck. I hummed against him. He tasted like the pure Castille soap I had detected on him as soon as I walked into the house. Almost all traces of Tyler's scent were gone.

I traveled to his collarbone after pulling his shirt down to expose it. The material needed to go. I sat back, straddled Patrick's hips, and pulled his shirt off over his head. Once his arms were free of the sleeves, Patrick placed his hands back against the headboard.

I growled and my canines descended. He was the picture of submission. I removed my shirt and flung it at a chair to the side of my bed. Patrick's gaze wandered up and down my chest.

I stroked my hands across his pecs, caressing them. They were smooth and muscular with only a dusting of hair. Patrick grunted and thrust his hips up as I pinched a nipple.

"Such a good Omega."

I descended on his mouth again, this time with more urgency, diving and thrusting with my tongue until we were both losing our breath.

I kissed a slow line from his chin to his abs, the whole journey matched by my fingers loosening his pants. When I had them open, I jerked them off his hips.

Patrick gasped and growled, squirming his bare ass into the bedding, his arms still above his head, his belly rising and falling rapidly, his breath close to panting.

This time when I licked his cock, it tasted purely of Patrick. I lingered as I ran my tongue up and down it, becoming familiar with its smooth skin and prominent veins. This was my fated mate's cock and I wanted to memorize every bit of it, so I could savor it in my mind later.

I held it firm in my fist until a bead of precum drooled down the side. I lapped it up and sucked his cock into my mouth. Patrick nearly hyperventilated, his breathing was so quick and shallow.

I placed my hand on his stomach to calm him. After his exhalations slowed and I satisfied myself with his cock, I whipped his pants off his legs to free them.

I stood at the side of the bed to remove mine, watching him studying me. It was a strange feeling. Not knowing each other—but also knowing each other so well. Knowing that our bodies would instinctively know what each other needed to feel fulfilled.

Patrick reached for me with such incredible desire in his eyes.

"Alpha," he whispered. I'd never tire of hearing that voice. Soft or loud. It was the voice of my Omega. The voice of my mate. I rejoined him on the bed, finding my place between his legs.

He was quick to wrap them around my waist.

His hands remained above his head.

I circled his hole with my thumb. It was dripping with slickness. I angled in against him and slid my cock into him. Again, that half howl—half curse erupted from his lips.

It was like a seductive carnal melody. My cock throbbed as I groaned and thrust, piercing Patrick as high as I could. I rocked back and thrust again, shifting Patrick up the bed.

He cried, "Yes, Alpha," and relaxed his arms, allowing them to rest softly on the pillow beneath his head. He looked like an angel nestled on a white cloud, my sweet, sweet, Omega.

His lips parted, and he grunted with each thrust, his tongue sometimes darting out. His gaze never left mine, like he was trying to see into my soul. I wanted to pour warmth into his.

He clung tighter to my waist with his legs, his heels bouncing off my ass cheeks.

"Ah," he mewled and licked his lips. "Please, Alpha, I need to seed."

He was asking permission. I nearly flooded him. I shifted so I could stroke his cheek. "Whenever you're ready, my precious Omega."

Patrick's eyelashes fluttered, he tipped his chin back, and his channel pulsed around my girth. He slapped his hands onto my shoulders, dug his fingernails in, and let his seed burst free.

After his body slowed, his seed coating his abs, he tightened his velvety hold on my cock. It pushed my body to react. I roared, feeling increasingly frenzied, as my cock knotted inside him.

"That's it, Alpha." Patrick relaxed his muscles. "Fill me with it." He touched my face. His features were barely distinguishable, I was so focused on my knot. "Stretch me wide, Alpha."

That cleared my vision.

I struggled, lifted Patrick's legs onto my shoulders, reset the position of my knees, and pulled out of him slightly, until I knew his hole would be burning. The pressure on the bulbous girth of my knot was incredible. I thrust back into him and then backed up, re-stretching him.

"Beautiful Omega," I cried and jammed up into him as my knot released. Each pulse filled him with enough seed to keep him slick for when I came back to him again later.

Patrick smiled up at me. "Told you I was going to spread out for you tonight."

I laughed and untangled his legs from off my shoulders. I lay down beside him, my softening cock becoming limp on my thigh. Patrick was quick to curl himself into my arms. He placed his head on my chest and brushed his fingers back and forth through the hair on my arm.

"You've rutted before," I said.

Patrick shifted and laughed against my skin. "Is it that obvious?"

"You know what you want." I played with his hair, inhaling the scent of it. I liked that my Omega was experienced. We were about the same age. Somewhere in our mid-30s. He'd likely seen as many Alphas as I had Omegas. Maybe he'd even rutted with Omegas as well.

I furrowed my brow.

Tyler.

Patrick had told me they'd never been intimate other than blow jobs. Which was strange enough as it was. They were two Omegas living and working together every day.

Surely their needs had taken them further than simply being on their knees.

He lifted his head and reached across me. "Could you pass me my wine?"

I grabbed the stem of his glass and passed it to him. He drained the wine from it and waggled the glass until I put it back on the bedside table.

"Tell me about your friends in Metro City," Patrick said.

I tugged him tighter to me. "Hm. Well, in the core group, there's Cindy—human. She's a graphic artist. Mostly commissions. Absolute wild card." I laughed. "Then there's Mario. Architect. Wolf. Wants to cover the world in tall glass and steel structures. Lance. Human. Unemployed most of the time. Apparently makes the best nachos."

"I've seen nachos. Lots of cheese."

I wrinkled my nose. "Tried cheese. Didn't like it."

"Who else?"

"I was in business with a human. Daniel. We got on well. I call him sometimes to see how he's doing." I smiled against Patrick's hair. "He got married. They have a baby now."

"Is that something you want?"

"To have a baby?"

Patrick laughed and shoved me. "No … a pup."

"Hadn't considered it until I met you."

"Now you want one?"

"I want as many as you're willing to have."

Patrick curled up against me, burying his face along my chin. His shoulders trembled, and his breath was hot against my skin. I might have upset him. I'd messed up somehow.

Did he not want pups?

"Have I said something wrong?" I asked.

"No. I'm just … I already …."

I rolled Patrick so I could see his face. It was tear-soaked and flushed. *I already* …. Two words I was afraid to know the meaning of. "Do you have pups already?"

It was a logical assumption.

"No … not mine."

"Then whose?"

"Tyler. He whelped three."

Still unclear. "Three of the four pups you were minding?"

Patrick sniffed and nodded.

"You need to back up," I said.

"Our friends, Harlan and Logan. Logan was past his breeding age, but they desperately wanted pups. Tyler volunteered to be their surrogate."

"He had the Alpha's pups? Did Tyler mate with him?" My hackles nearly went up. For some reason, the thought of Tyler mating with an Alpha who was already mated upset me.

"No, we used a human method. A whole long uncomfortable procedure at a fertility clinic in Metro City.

Three embryos were viable. Tyler decided to have all three of them implanted."

"Three is a lot of pups for a wolf to carry to term."

"Tyler suffered a lot of discomfort throughout the entire pregnancy."

I feared I knew where this was going.

"Were you about to say you already have pups?"

Patrick exhaled a heavy breath. "They're my family."

"You, Tyler, and the pups?"

Patrick simply nodded. I wasn't sure what this meant for us. How this would affect our future moving forward with our own family. I had one other question.

"Are you in love with Tyler?"

This time a shuddering whine shook Patrick's body. He looked up at me, searching my eyes for a way out of the question, beseeching me to withdraw it.

I refused to do so.

"Patrick, please … I need to know."

Patrick ducked his gaze away and stared at my chest.

"We're in love," he whispered.

My heart nearly stopped. Love was an emotion we were supposed to be headed for. What would happen if Patrick already loved another? Would he have room in his heart for me?

"Do you want to be with him? To be his mate?"

"I wanted that for *so many* years." Patrick raised his head and his gaze locked on mine. "Then I met you and my world changed. We're fated. Someday I'll love you too."

"But never as much as Tyler?"

Patrick released a puffing breath out through his nose. "I don't honestly know. What I have with Tyler runs deep, but maybe someday my love for you will eclipse my love for Tyler."

"I don't think that's likely."

"Why do you say that?"

"Because … you have a family with him. You're bound to him by that."

Patrick blinked at me and then lowered his gaze. "I love what Tyler and I have together."

My next words were going to make my heart ache, but I didn't want to lose my fated mate. Pushing him to commit to me when he loved another might make him walk away from me. I wanted my Omega to be happy and fulfilled. I couldn't ask him to abandon his family.

"I don't want to take you away from that. My heart has already started to beat for you, but I don't want you to leave your family behind for me. I would never ask you to do that."

Patrick's eyebrows furrowed as he looked at me.

"What does that mean?"

"It means I'd like you to split your time between your family and me for now. Maybe when we start having our own pups, we'll have to rethink things, but I want you to go to him. Keep loving him. Keep loving your pups." Tears formed in my eyes. I meant what I said. My fated mate was capable of incredible love. He had chosen to reveal his love for another. What he and Tyler shared must be incredibly special. His commitment to his family wrapped me in warmth.

My Omega was a complex, loving, and loyal wolf.

He was everything I had ever dreamed would be present in my fated mate.

It would be a short trip to fall in love with him.

Chapter Five | Patrick

Declan had offered me a gift. A chance to explore my love for Tyler. I wanted to grasp onto it and run with it, but I was worried. What if Tyler and I sank deeper into our love and Declan changed his mind? Would I be able to defy the needs of my fated mate?

Because—at this point—my heart belonged to Tyler alone. I knew that would change. Fated mates were destined for each other. Declan and I would naturally fall in love at some point.

I knew in my heart, though, that my love for Tyler was absolute.

What if Tyler found his fated mate? Could we fight the pull to leave each other behind?

Could I stand the heartbreak if Tyler and I were forced to go our separate ways?

The thought of any of those scenarios terrified me.

"I love him deeply," I said.

"I understand that."

"You would be all right with me mating with Tyler?"

Declan kissed my forehead. "You're in love. I wouldn't deny you mating with him."

The potential of the whole arrangement nearly made my mind explode with possibilities. It also endeared Declan to me. I had never expected my fated mate to be so open.

I sat up, rolled onto my knee, and straddled Declan's hips. I desperately needed him to mate with me again. He closed his eyes and growled softly as I lifted his soft cock.

Stroking its length, it soon hardened.

I shifted forward and sat fully on his cock, making Declan groan. Rise and fall, I watched his changing expressions. He was a handsome wolf. Sexy and stoic packaged up together.

I bounced faster, ensuring I ran his cock over my sensitive gland buried inside. Beyond that, the path leading to my cervix. The right angle would have it being seeded heavily.

I was due for another heat soon, but mating with my fated mate might bring it on as early as tonight. My body would be primed to receive my mate's seed and produce a pup.

I wasn't sure I wanted that.

I placed my hands on Declan's chest and rocked my hips, bouncing his cock off my prostate until I couldn't contain my climax. I wouldn't ask permission this time. This time, I was in charge.

I grunted, stilled my hips, and stroked my cock, my breath catching in my throat.

The first rope of my seed landed on my mate's chest. His fingers were immediately in it, smearing it across his skin as the second wave hit me. I threw my head back and howled, my hand tight on my cock as I coated his belly in pulsing bursts of my ecstasy.

His seed-covered hands came to rest on my hips. I grabbed one, brought it to my mouth, and sucked on his fingers, moaning as I reveled in the familiar taste.

Declan pumped his hips up and down, pistoning into me, jarring my body. I rode every thrust and retreat, tightening my channel around his cock. A rush of warmth swept across my forehead.

As I suspected, my body was on the verge of a heat.

I met every penetration by taking it as high as I could, my lashes fluttering, barely aware of the room, Declan's fingers riding my tongue.

He howled and jammed his hips up. I knew he was filling me. I wanted more. I wanted him to mate with me all night. I collapsed on his chest after releasing his fingers from my mouth.

Declan's body shook as he laughed.

"You definitely know what you want," he said.

"You'll find I'm not shy."

"Good. I wouldn't want you to be."

I kissed him. I wasn't ready to perform the claiming ceremony with him yet, but every moment I spent with him was bringing me closer to wanting that.

The rest of the night, we barely slept, we were so consumed with each other. The bedding turned into a patchwork of wet spots. Come morning, we continued mating in the shower.

It was hard to drag myself away from Declan, but I needed to head to work. Our Monday morning schedule was a busy one. I made good time, but I was 20 minutes late.

Tyler was beneath a car doing an oil change when I walked into the garage.

"Good morning," I said.

Tyler grunted in response and kept working on the car. We needed to have a conversation but now wasn't the time. Maybe tonight after work. I wouldn't be going to Declan tonight.

That's the conversation we needed to have.

"Has my brake job been dropped off yet?" I asked.

Tyler's hands stopped moving, then he dropped them to his sides. He turned to face me. His nose was red, and his cheeks and lips were coated in tears.

I rushed to his side.

"Tyler, talk to me."

More tears streamed down his cheeks. "You smell like his seed."

"He's my fated mate. We mated last night."

"Maybe a shower was in order."

"We did … mated there too."

Tyler turned and rushed across the garage away from me. "I don't think I can do this."

I chased him into the office. "Do what?"

Tyler spun on me; his face twisted with despair. "Work with you."

"What? No, Tyler. You can't take off on me like that."

"The business will be fine. I'll apprentice for a different job."

I grabbed his arm. "Absolutely not. I would give this place up if you left."

"That's ridiculous. This business belonged to your sire."

"This is *our* business now. *Creekside Motors* wouldn't exist without you."

"Are you trying to guilt me into staying?"

I released his arm. "Of course not."

"*Creekside Motors* will continue to thrive without me." Tyler placed his hand on my chest. "I love you, Patrick. I can't stand to have his scent all over you."

"I'll shower alone from now on."

"That won't help, and you know it. You're filled with his seed."

I turned away from him. I hadn't completely considered what Declan had suggested. Of course, Tyler wouldn't want to be intimate with me if I carried Declan's scent.

Now, he didn't even want to work with me.

Our conversation wouldn't be happening the way I had intended. If he couldn't stand to work with me, how would he feel about me sleeping in the same room as him?

I'd have to move in with Harlan and Logan.

The sound of Tyler whining behind me made me turn around. His arms were limp by his sides, the pale blue of his eyes glistening with fresh tears as he stared at me.

"I can't …," he whispered. "I can't leave you."

I wandered closer to him. "What does that mean?'

"It means I need you to hold me." He stepped into my outstretched arms and clung to me, sobbing. I wanted us to morph into one being as we held one another.

I reached out to him through our pack telepathic connection.

Me: "I love you."

Tyler: "I never thought I'd ever love like this."

Me: "It hurts."

Tyler nodded against my shoulder.

Tyler: "I want to spend every moment kissing you. Having you hold me."

I kissed his head with my tear-dampened lips.

Me: "Let me. Let me keep holding you."

Tyler: "You can't. You're not mine."

Me: "I want to be. Please let me."

Tyler looked up at me. "What are you saying?"

"Declan doesn't believe I should abandon you or our family."

Tyler took a step back. "You told him about us?"

"We were talking about pups. It triggered me. I ended up telling him I'm in love with you and that I cherish the family we've created together."

Tyler didn't speak for far too long.

"And he's all right with that?" he said at last.

"He says it's my choice what I want to do." I gathered Tyler up in my arms again. "If you'll have me, I want to spend time with you too. I want us to be a mated pair."

"You want us to be mated?"

"I want to love you in every way possible." I cupped Tyler's face and pulled him away from my shoulder. I set my lips on his, sinking into a depth of unprecedented emotional union.

My love for Tyler was stunning.

He stroked his fingers into my hair and caressed his tongue between my lips. We both groaned as I backed him against the filing cabinet. Over the years, we'd spent hours in that office pleasuring each other. I didn't want what was happening between us now to be *that*.

We were both panting as we pulled apart.

"Wrong time and place," Tyler said.

"I was thinking the same thing."

"We should finish our day."

"Unfortunately." I reluctantly released Tyler. Concentrating on today's jobs was going to be difficult. I wanted his beautiful nude body above me. I'd seen him naked many times. Getting out of the shower. Dressing and undressing in our room. I'd dreamed of having his skin on mine.

Tonight, we'd be sharing a bed for the first time.

We'd be sharing our bodies.

My cock thickened as I walked out to the garage, imaging how we would fit together. I wanted Tyler's seed in me; the seed of the wolf I loved beyond any earthly measure.

I finished my brake job and went into our convenience store for coffee. I poured one for Tyler and myself. He took his dark brew black. Without contaminants—his words.

I found him in front of the large red toolbox, polishing a wrench from one of the drawers. He was fastidious when it came to his tools. It was one of the things I loved about him.

I set his coffee on the workbench beside him.

He smiled at me. "Thanks."

I leaned closer to him. His smile grew wider, and he licked his lips as I closed in. He caught my lips with his. I pressed my body against him, my cock becoming curious.

"Well … this is a new development."

I laughed and pulled away from Tyler.

Logan.

I'd forgotten he was coming in this afternoon. I turned and leaned my ass against Tyler. He wrapped his arms around my waist and kissed the back of my neck.

"You two finally together?" Logan said, smirking. "It's about time."

"We were stubborn," Tyler replied, his fingers gripping my coveralls. His touch reminded me that tonight his hands were going to be all over my body.

"Felt like it was time to tell this gorgeous wolf I'm in love with him," I said.

"I'm thrilled for you," Logan replied. "Harlan not so much. He just lost some money."

Tyler's chest rose and fell behind me as he laughed. "You bet on us?"

"I told him it was just a matter of time. He wasn't convinced after you two seemed to be so close during the pregnancy and then nothing happened between you."

"There was a lot going on," Tyler said. "My hormones were messing with my head. I knew I was in love with Patrick. More so every day … he was so supportive, but I didn't know what I wanted from him. All I knew was that those pups were coming. I was focused on them."

I reached back for Tyler's thigh and held it. "We've figured it out now."

I could see that Logan was inhaling longer breaths. His eyes narrowed as he looked at me. He'd detected Declan's seed on me. It was none of his business—but ....

"I found my fated mate," I said.

"That makes no sense to me." Logan tipped his head to one side. "Shouldn't you be with him?"

"I was ... now, I'm spending time with Tyler."

"And your Alpha is all right with that?"

"He is. He suggested it."

Logan shook his head. "I could never share my mate."

"Declan and I will be spending a lot of time checking in," I replied. We had agreed to keep communication open about Tyler. I would be doing the same with Tyler.

"Mark's brother, Declan? The leader of the Riverton pack?"

"I picked *Cooper Accounting* to do our bookkeeping and taxes," Tyler said. "My luck, my laziness landed us in the path of Patrick's fated mate."

"You would have detected him on Mark eventually," Logan said to me.

"Declan and Mark don't see each other often." Declan had told me he and Mark had a difference of opinion on how Mark had governed the pack; often devolving into an argument.

Declan's ruling style was different. He had spent the last seven years cultivating a core group of the pack who were the main governing party. Each one represented a family unit. Most things would go to vote but ultimately, Declan had the final say. Turning the pack away from its antiquated ways had been difficult to achieve. It had taken years of debating the benefits of change.

My fated mate seemed more than capable of leading a pack.

Someday, I would join him in that leadership.

Right now, though, I was with Tyler. This was our time together. Declan could have me back tomorrow night. Logan lost interest in us and wandered over to his end of the garage. He had three motorcycles he was working on, including one I had picked up to restore recently.

Tyler gripped my shoulders and turned me to face him.

"One more kiss and then back to work," he said.

"Mm ... let's make it a good one."

Tyler's nose wrinkled as he grinned and placed his forehead on mine. "I love you."

"I love you too."

I descended on his lips. He hummed and growled as I kissed him, filling my throat with a vibrating sound. It traveled straight to my cock. I pinned him to the workbench.

Tyler slapped his hands on my shoulders and pushed me away.

He smirked at me.

"We are *not* going to get any work done if we keep getting distracted like this."

"You're no fun."

"Oh ... I will be plenty of fun when we get home tonight."

I groaned and left him clinging to the workbench. I had an exhaust system to replace this afternoon. Tyler had drawn the short straw, relegated to oil changes today.

I'd never been as happy to close the bay doors as I was that night. We were able to knock off a bit early because I had come in yesterday before heading to Declan's. I had worked on a few of the cars that had been scheduled for today. Shutting down the garage almost seemed surreal.

Tonight had significance.

We took Tyler's truck back to the house. It wasn't on our minds to feed before retreating to our bedroom. Our attention during the drive home was locked on each other.

We held hands the whole way.

After engaging in a spattering of small talk with our housemates, we excused ourselves. During the day, our flirtations had been playful. Now, we were silent as I closed our door.

Tyler sat on the end of his bed and reached for me. I wandered into the space between his legs and stroked the hair above his ears. He melted against my hand as I cradled his face.

I brushed his skin with my thumb. "My beautiful Omega."

Tyler's lips parted. "Love me, Omega."

"Always."

I started with his shirt, removing it, and tossed it onto my bed. The skin of his shoulders and chest reflected the light from the small bedside lamp. My gaze wandered to the tattoo he had on his ribcage. While he'd been pregnant, it had stretched. I'd bought special oil for Tyler to rub into it to keep it supple. It was back to being solid black and perfect, wrapping around his left side.

Tyler rose to his feet and stripped off my shirt. We stood staring into each others' eyes in silence. In the past, there had always been a stream of banter before a blow job.

This was so much more than that.

We were in love.

Tyler's hands trembled as he fumbled with the front of my jeans. He squatted and dragged them down my legs once he had them freed, then ascended to slowly take my mouth.

He took his time. We were in no rush.

The humans called it *making love*. That's what we were doing. This wasn't rutting. This wasn't even mating. There was no drive for pups. There was just us—together, sharing our love.

He yanked his pants off his hips, sat on the bed, and pulled them from his legs. I licked my lips, my gaze wandering over his nude body; my hands trembled at the sight of him.

Tyler was ethereal.

He backed his ass up the bed until he was able to lay his head on his pillow.

"Come to me, Omega," he whispered.

I crawled up his body until I was kneeling, straddling his thighs, my hard cock suspended between us. I was in the perfect place to kiss him again. This time he was against a firm surface. Our tongues tangled and danced together as I pinned him against his pillow with my mouth.

He moaned, writhed beneath me, and placed his hands on my hips. I lowered my ass onto his thighs. My cock came to rest on his. Tyler moved one of his hands off my hip and gripped both our shafts in a firm grasp. He slipped his hand up and down and I nearly passed out.

It was the most sublime sensation I'd ever experienced.

I moaned softly as Tyler pumped our joined cocks.

I brushed my thumbs across his nipples. Memories of when he fed the pups for those many weeks surfaced. His nipples had become pink and puffy, his pecs soft-looking.

I abandoned Tyler's grip on my cock and shuffled down Tyler's body. After kissing his collarbone, I sucked one of his firm nipples into my mouth.

Tyler groaned and grabbed the back of my head to hold me in place. He rocked his hips up beneath me. His cock pressed into my abs, distracting me for a second. I kissed his sternum and had my full taste of his skin, licking his flesh as I descended.

His familiar cock was soon in my mouth, riding my tongue. I knew every surface of his warm velvety skin intimately. I knew what he liked. What would drive him wild with lust.

Once I had his cock straining, I found his mouth again, this time holding his chin. His gaze was fixed on mine. There was pure love radiating from his eyes.

"I want you to fill me with your seed," I said.

Tyler blinked. "I've never done that before."

I gave him a quick kiss and smiled at him. "I'm sure we can figure it out."

Tyler bit his bottom lip as he looked at me. "My scent will be mixed with Declan's."

"It will."

Tyler mewled, grabbed my ass, and undulated his hips up, jamming his cock against me.

"Does that turn you on?" I asked.

Tyler blushed fiercely but nodded his head. He rolled me. I almost fell off the side of the twin-sized bed. We shuffled around until I was under him. He hovered above my lips.

"My Omega," he said.

"All yours," I responded. It was the truth. For tonight, I was all Tyler's. Every piece of me. No one else mattered. Not the world. Not my fated mate. I was Tyler's alone.

I separated my legs and wrapped them around his waist. The change of position had the scent of Declan's seed wafting up between us. Tyler growled and attacked my mouth.

After ravaging my lips, Tyler found a spot behind my ear to flood me with his hot breath. He nibbled, sucked, and used his teeth to pull on my earlobe. His canines had descended.

He repositioned his cock, using his hand to guide it to my hole. I clung to his broad shoulders. Tears collected in my eyes as Tyler slipped past my outer ring and entered my body.

Not tears of pain—tears of joy.

Tyler drove his cock home, his thick girth filling me. We were as close as any two wolves could be. He pumped his hips—slow and easy. I brushed my hand down his spine.

He was crying too.

I held his head in both hands and brought his face back to focus on mine. We were both a mess of tears. I brought his mouth down to mine. Our lips were damp and salty.

I concentrated on the feel of Tyler's breathing, his belly, and mine in sync. With each thrust, his abs would clench. I ran my hands onto his ass, riding the rhythm of his hips.

His mouth free to wander, Tyler made his way to my claiming area between my neck and shoulder. He licked and sucked it. I was overcome with emotion.

"I want to be yours," Tyler said.

My heart soared. Claiming each other had been a dream I never thought would transpire in the real world. My mind briefly flitted to Declan. I wasn't in love with him.

"And I yours," I responded.

I cried, "Yes, Omega," as Tyler's canines pierced my skin. It burned. He sucked a few times and then returned to my mouth. My blood on his lips tasted pleasantly of iron.

My canines ached as I positioned myself. I sank my teeth into Tyler's claiming area and sucked hard. A new level of telepathic consciousness between us shimmered to life.

I had access to his emotions.

We shared the beauty of them. The beauty of our love.

I released him but kept clinging to him. His abs rippled against me as he drove his cock harder into me. I clamped my channel down on him. Released and clamped again.

Tyler swore in my ear and growled, deep and throaty.

The vibrating, possessive sound made my cock pulse.

I felt his body tense.

He tugged on my earlobe, whispered "I love you," and flooded me with seed. He rocked his hips, slipping his cock in and out of me. His cock stayed firm enough to drag across my gland.

He looked down at me, reacting to every emotion on my face as he drove me closer to climax. With each thrust, I grunted. Sometimes closing my eyes. Until I remembered, I needed to stay connected to him. I licked my lips, lifted my chin, and mewled softly as I painted my stomach with my seed. Tyler coaxed every drop from me as he licked and sucked on my lips.

Both spent, Tyler slid to the side of me, his chest pressed to my arm. We squirmed around until Tyler was in my arms. I started the claiming howl deep in my chest.

Tyler joined me and we sang a haunting song of intense love and commitment.

The rest of the house joined us.

No one interrupted our thoughts as we finished the song to find out when the change in our relationship had happened. I doubted anyone would be overly surprised.

I tugged Tyler closer to me.

We were claimed mates.

I wasn't sure how Declan would feel about that.

I kissed Tyler's head.

For now, I was going to savor our love.

Chapter Six | Tyler

I snuggled against the side of my claimed mate. My Patrick. He had told me what we were doing was *making love*. It fit with how I felt. I'd been flooding him with love all night.

Patrick had fallen into a deep sleep early this morning.

My mind wouldn't let me rest.

I was concerned about Patrick returning to Declan tonight. It was obvious we had claimed each other. Not sure that's what Declan meant when he told Patrick he could come to me.

When he'd said Patrick wouldn't be expected to give up the wolf he loved.

I kissed Patrick's shoulder. He made a few mumbling noises. I was used to him talking in his sleep. We'd been sharing a room for almost twenty years.

That number was mind-boggling.

So much wasted time.

Some part of me had always loved Patrick. But it hadn't crossed into romantic feelings until I'd been pregnant with the triplets six years ago. He'd been so loving toward me.

I closed my eyes, letting a memory wash over me. Sometimes when Patrick had been in my bed rubbing my back, I'd been awoken by him kissing the back of my head.

He'd thought I was asleep.

Instead, he'd brought me close to tears.

I'd shoved my feelings for him down. He'd continued to be so sweet to me. But we were two Omegas. Despite being so attentive, I'd believed Patrick could never be mine.

My thoughts had always drawn me toward his ultimate happiness. I knew in my heart that one day Patrick would find his fated mate. I didn't want to be an obstacle to that union.

Now, that's exactly what I was doing—what we were doing.

"Tyler." Patrick's voice was rough. "Did you sleep?"

"Too much going on in my head."

"You thinking about us?"

"Can't stop. Do you think Declan will be upset?"

"That we claimed each other? I think I'm about to find out he would have preferred if he and I had gone through the ceremony first."

"I don't like the idea of him claiming you." I wasn't sure if it was jealousy or pure and simple possessiveness. Patrick was mine and I was his for life now. No wolf would dare pull us apart.

Someone like Declan, being the leader of a pack, could make things difficult for us, though. I knew nothing about him. If he ordered Patrick to abandon me, Patrick would have to fight hard to defy him and keep our relationship intact. I stroked his arm with my fingers.

My mate was strong enough to protect our love.

"I won't have a choice," Patrick replied. "Declan is my fated mate. We're destined to claim each other. We're destined to fall in love." Patrick entwined his fingers with mine. "Doesn't negate anything you and I have together. You will always be my genuine love uninfluenced by fate."

"I'm going to love you forever."

Patrick kissed my forehead. "Sweet, Omega. I'll be by your side the whole time."

I rolled Patrick away from me and kissed the back of his neck. Kissing became licking. Licking became growling and sucking. My hard cock speared the space between his thighs.

He shifted his ass, clinging to the sheets, and with one hand gripping my cock, I thrust into him.

Holding his hip and gnawing his shoulder, we reached a howling climax together.

THE GARAGE WAS BUSY today. We had a couple of people with flat tires in addition to our regular scheduled work. Usually, we would have the gas jockey deal with the flat tires, but he was covering the pumps and the store. Today's clerk had called in sick at the last moment. A replacement was coming but not until she could find a babysitter.

Our staff consisted of all humans. Mostly much younger than us, including a couple of teenagers who had been looking for weekend work. We tried to treat our employees well. Their wages were more than competitive even though we were the only gas station in town. We'd decided on providing health benefits for the full-time employees and two paid weeks off a year.

Our business was doing well. We had a significant amount of money sitting in our business savings account. Patrick wanted to expand. Add another bay to the garage and renovate the store. It was showing its years of service. Patrick wanted to incorporate a fast-food restaurant.

We were alone in the garage. Logan had gone to *Growlers* for a feed. Patrick was leaning over a car working on the alternator. I wandered over to him and ran my hand down his ass.

Patrick groaned, set his tool on the fuse box, and turned to face me. He reached for me and brought our lips together. I inhaled the profuse scent of him. There was an intoxicating mix of seeds in the forefront. Mine overpowering the waning scent of Declan's.

Patrick's fated mate would know I had truly claimed him as mine.

I was looking forward to having Patrick return to me after a night with Declan.

The thought made my cock hard.

I pressed it against Patrick's thickening girth. "Office," I growled.

Yesterday, the office had been out of the question. We needed our first time to be special. And it had been the most incredible experience of my life. We'd been overflowing with love.

Right now—this was about carnal need.

Patrick dashed into the office with me close behind. We remembered to lock the door. Patrick struggled out of his coveralls, shoved his jeans and underwear around his ankles, and supported himself on the filing cabinet, ass poised for me. I brushed my hand across his round flesh.

His ass was beautiful.

I slipped my finger down his crease to his hole and found him slick and wet. I unsnapped my coveralls and opened my jeans enough to expose my hard cock.

I slid into him in one smooth motion.

He banged on the filing cabinet and swore. I clung to his waist as I thrust into him, jamming higher and higher. Patrick liked extreme penetration. It coiled him up, ready to spring free.

I grunted and hammered into him harder.

"Oh, god ... yes!" spilled from Patrick's mouth.

Too loud. Someone might hear us. I clapped my hand over his mouth. That seemed to turn him on. He moaned and whined against my hand. I wrapped my other arm around his chest and clung to his pec. I was able to reach the side of his neck with my mouth.

I sucked hard, leaving a purpling mark among all the others I had given him all over his body.

Those possessive marks and the bruises on his inner thighs.

My claiming bite.

There would be no question. Patrick was mine.

I changed my rhythm, building Patrick up. From this angle, I was dragging my cock over his gland. He dropped his ass onto my cock, bouncing on it. It sent tingles through my balls. My mouth dropped open; all the air inflating my lungs ceased—and we released our seed as one.

A few slow thrusts and I collapsed on Patrick's back. He'd be leaving me soon. Tears formed in my eyes as I hugged him. "Promise me you'll come back to me."

"Hey …." Patrick struggled away from my embrace and turned around to face me. "You have nothing to worry about. Even Declan can't stop me from being with you now."

"I want to believe that."

"I'll be here at work in the morning. Same as always. We can take a moment to reconnect." Patrick's gaze flicked up toward the clock on the wall. "Another couple of hours, then I need to leave. I want to be at Declan's by 5 tonight. I'd like to hunt for some rabbits."

"He gave you hunting rights?"

"I'm the leader's fated mate. My rights are automatic."

An image of Patrick taking his spot at Declan's side during a conflict slammed itself into my mind. They would be equal partners when it came to leadership.

Patrick would be in a position of power.

It made me feel better.

He wouldn't abandon me.

THE MOONLIGHT LIT MY WAY up the driveway to the East Creekside pack's compound. It had been years since we'd needed to secure permission to be on the property. We crossed into their territory at least twice a week visiting Harlan, Logan, and the pups.

Tonight, I needed to be surrounded by our pups.

I'd kissed Patrick goodbye and he'd taken off for Declan's.

I'd called ahead and talked to Harlan. We didn't usually visit at night. I'd explained I needed to be surrounded by the love of the pups—and to talk to him and Logan.

I heard screeching before the door was even opened. It swung open, held by a dishevelled-looking Logan. He ran his hand through his hair and stepped back to let me in.

"I don't know how the pup sitter does it," he said. "I've been home less than two hours."

"I don't mind taking over," I replied.

Logan patted my shoulder. "You're a godsend."

"Where's Harlan?"

"In the garage. Big job tomorrow. He's fretting over supplies."

Rose went streaking past me, Reese close on her heels. Harlan and Logan's house, inadvertent in its design, had a perfect circuit built into it. One big circle. Kitchen to front hall to living room to dining room and back to the kitchen. Haley and Harry dashed past next.

I caught Rose under her arms as she made her next round. "All right. That's enough for tonight." I lifted her onto one hip and stood in the way of Reese's path.

"Papa Tyler is right," Logan said. "It's time for bed."

A collective, "Awe," made me smile.

"Two stories tonight," I said. I wanted to spend as much time as I could with them. We would read the stories in Harry and Reese's room. Rose and Haley were more trustworthy when it came to heading straight to their bedroom after the stories. Harry and Reese tended to get distracted.

"I bathed them already," Logan said.

"Perfect." I looked appreciative but inside, I was disappointed. Bathtime was fun. They had some cool toys. The latest were little letters that stuck to the tiles where they could practice spelling their first words. Harry was lagging. He struggled with a lot of things. He'd been the smallest of the three pups when I whelped them. He'd never caught up. He was a spitfire, though.

"Okay, I'm going to time you," I said. "I have a sticker for whoever is the fastest to put on their pajamas and brush their teeth." I always carried stickers in my wallet for such occasions.

"Bribery," Logan said, laughing. "Always a winner."

I shoved him. "Go sit down. I've got this."

Logan sighed. "Thanks, Tyler. We'll talk when you're done."

Once Logan was headed for the family room, I mounted the stairs. There was a flurry of activity happening upstairs. A fight was about to break out in front of the sink.

Minor casualties were acceptable.

I waited for them to pile into the bedroom. According to the chart on the wall, it was Reese's turn to pick the stories. That would open a debate. Reese was obsessed with dinosaurs.

As predicted, he picked two dinosaur books.

There was a unanimous groan.

I flipped the book back and forth. At least this was a new one. I opened the first page and realized there wouldn't be anyone to speak in funny character voices.

Patrick and I always read books to the pups together.

He was the wolf with the voices they loved so much.

I did my best. I kept mixing the voices up which prompted giggling protests and a lot of jubilant corrections. At least the pups had a good sense of humor.

After the two stories, I tucked Harry and Reese in and kissed their little cheeks, and herded Rose and Haley into their bedroom. Rose pulled the blanket up under her chin.

"Where's Uncle Patrick?"

I brushed her curls away from her eyes. "He has a fated mate."

"Does that mean he won't play with us anymore?" Haley asked.

"No." I shook my head. "Of course he will. Your Uncle Patrick loves you."

"Then why isn't he here?" Rose asked.

"Well." I crossed my arms. "Uncle Patrick wants to have more pups like you because he loves you all so much. He has to spend time with his fated mate to do that."

"We'll have brothers and sisters?" Haley asked.

"Hopefully."

Any more talk of Patrick having pups and I was liable to start crying. He'd admitted to me last night that he'd wished he could have been the one to give me the triplets.

His words had stuck with me.

I patted Rose's blankets. "Okay. Bed." I leaned down and kissed her forehead. She was so blonde, I liked to think she *was* Patrick's. Haley got a special butterfly kiss tonight.

Haley had won the bedtime race. She had a sticker in her sweaty little palm, and she'd requested that I flutter my eyelashes on her cheek as her nighttime kiss.

I turned off the light and pulled the door until it was almost closed.

I could hear Harlan and Logan talking in the family room. I made a pass through the kitchen first. Predictably, there was a bottle of wine open on the counter. I poured myself a glass.

They'd left the comfy recliner vacant for me.

Harlan was practically sitting in Logan's lap. Their age difference was becoming more prominent as each year passed. Logan's trimmed beard was speckled with grey and white hairs.

At twenty-six, Harlan still looked like a kid.

They were the best friends, other than Patrick, that I'd ever had.

"I'm going to guess this has something to do with Patrick," Harlan said. "Judging by his absence tonight."

"He's with Declan tonight," I replied.

"So ... what exactly is the arrangement?" Logan asked.

"Right now, he's going to alternate his nights." I took a sip of my wine. It sounded outrageous to say aloud. The couple sitting across from me thought so too.

Harlan waved his hand as he swallowed his wine. "So, he *is* mating with you both."

I rubbed the side of my neck. I wanted them to have the full picture. I pulled the neck of my shirt down to expose the bite mark where Patrick had claimed me.

Logan leaned forward. "Oh ... shit. You claimed each other?"

"Declan is not going to like that," Harlan added. "He's liberal but he's also an Alpha leader."

"It felt destined," I said. "Not sure we could have stopped ourselves."

"You really are in love," Harlan said.

I stared into my wine glass. "You have no idea."

Harlan reached for and took Logan's hand. "I think we have some idea."

I looked up at them. "It's different. You're fated. Our love grew from our long friendship." I couldn't explain it. I knew fated love was strong but ours had so many more layers.

Patrick was right. It hurt it was so strong.

"I *am* worried," I said.

"About what happens when Patrick and Declan do claim each other," Logan replied.

"It would make sense for Patrick to move in with Declan."

"Would he give up the business?" Harlan asked.

"Right now, I think he thinks he wouldn't. But he's not there yet—in love."

Harlan set down his empty wine glass. "That's got to hurt. Knowing someday he's going to love somebody else too. I can't imagine what that would feel like."

"It's heartbreaking—trust me."

Logan stared at me for a few moments. "I think his heart will always be yours. I see the way you two are together. I've been witness to it for years. His love for you is endless." He clasped his hands together. "Moving forward, let's go with the information we have today. Patrick loves you and the pups and the life you've built together, right?"

"Yes."

"And he's promised to spend workdays and every second night with you."

"Right."

"And supposedly, the arrangement was Declan's idea."

"That's what Patrick told me."

"I can't see that Declan wouldn't anticipate you claiming each other," Harlan said. "What did he think he was agreeing to? You're two wolves in love who have the urge to mate."

"Claiming Patrick as mine might have been a step too far," I replied, then looked at my hands, and smirked. "And I may have returned him slightly damaged."

Harlan snorted. "What did you do?"

"Let's just say, Patrick has an assortment of marks all over his body."

"Pure evil."

I raised my gaze. Logan was grinning at me after speaking.

I leaned back in the recliner. "We'll know by tomorrow morning, but I suspect Patrick will be bearing some more mating marks, but from Declan. He'll see what I did as a challenge."

"Poor Patrick," Harlan said.

"Poor Patrick nothing," I replied. "He loves it."

Logan raised both hands. "Too much information."

The rest of the evening unfolded more sedately. My hosts started to drop off around 9. We all had early starts, and they had pups to wrangle in the morning.

I fell asleep alone in bed that night dreaming of Patrick.

And the marks from Declan I'd need to kiss better.

Chapter Seven | Declan

I sat in my car, staring at my house. It was once again lit by warm light. I could hear music playing. But it was the scent of my fated mate that was giving me pause.

It was laced heavily with the scent of Tyler's seed.

They'd mated.

My cock stirred as I thought about them together. I wished I knew what Tyler looked like. Right now, he was faceless. Patrick had only told me Tyler wore his dark blond hair combed back in the style of a 50s greaser and that he preferred to travel by motorcycle. Classic bad boy.

I shifted in my seat. My cock had swelled. I needed to go inside.

I slammed my car door and jogged up the front steps. As I opened the door, the full scent of Tyler's seed inside my mate assaulted me. A growl built in my chest.

Not a growl of aggression. A growl of intense desire.

"Omega."

Patrick's head popped up above the back of the sofa. He had been lying down. Maybe he'd been up all night mating with Tyler. He looked tired. He remained stretched out on the sofa.

"Alpha."

My growl came out this time, rumbling, as I surged into the living room. I wasn't interested in his lips tonight. I unlatched and jerked Patrick's pants and underwear off his hips.

He chewed on his bottom lip as he lifted his feet so I could take his bottoms off completely. I ran my hands up his legs from his ankles to his thighs. He sighed and opened his legs.

My fingers stopped on a yellow and purple mark on his inner thigh. My cock pulsed. Tyler had been hammering into my mate with some force to leave a bruise like that. There was a matching one on the other side. I sank to my knees, leaned forward, and kissed the marks.

The scent of Tyler was so incredibly strong there.

"How long ago did you mate with him?"

"Ah ... I don't know. About 5 hours ago."

I groaned. Patrick would still be damp with him. "On your knees. Face the back of the sofa."

Patrick sat up, rolled onto his knees, and clung to the upholstery. He swayed his back, jamming his ass into the air, and separated his legs. He knew exactly what I wanted.

I brushed my fingers across Patrick's skin. More bruises. Contact spots from where Tyler's hipbones had slammed against my mate's flesh. And three purple oblong blotches.

Tyler had sucked on Patrick's ass until he made those marks.

I stroked his ass cheeks and kissed his tailbone as I inhaled the incredible scent emanating from his hole. I used my thumbs to expose it and licked his ridged flesh.

I quivered with ecstasy.

I could taste Tyler's seed on him. I sucked and licked, and jammed my tongue as far into his hole as I could manage. Patrick moaned and pushed his ass toward me. I buried my face between Patrick's ass cheeks, immersing myself in the tantalizing taste and scent.

I dipped my tongue deeper into his hole, encouraging the tight ring to relax. I retreated enough that I could press my finger inside him. My finger withdrawn went straight into my mouth.

I groaned as my eyes rolled back; overwhelmed by my new lust-fueled addiction.

I rose to my feet, fumbled with my pants, and exposed my rock-hard cock. I hauled Patrick closer to the edge of the sofa and thrust into him. Patrick rocked back to enhance the jostling effect of my hips. I pumped into him as high as I could manage, making him groan and pant.

It didn't take me long.

Tyler's scent mixed with Patrick's was still on my lips.

I licked them.

Oh, God ....

I growled and unleashed rapid surges of seed into my fated mate. I kept pumping. I couldn't stop until I stumbled backward, my knees weak. I plopped down on the coffee table and studied Patrick's ass. From this angle, I could see all the marks Tyler had left on him.

I suspected there were more.

"Turn around and slip your shirt off for me," I said.

As Patrick followed my directions, I leaned forward.

You've got to be kidding me.

I smiled as I examined Patrick's skin. He had a hickey on the soft part of his stomach, one shoulder, his chest, and his neck. And one of his nipples looked like it had seen too much attention.

Tyler was growing on me.

"We might have got a little carried away," Patrick said and smirked at me.

I growled and launched myself at his lips. Before I contacted them, I caught a glimpse of a crescent-shaped bite mark on the claiming area on his left side.

I fell to my knees in front of him.

"You claimed each other?"

"We're in love. If we were an Alpha and an Omega, we would be claimed mates." Patrick cupped my face in one hand. "I need you to understand how much Tyler means to me."

I stroked my fingers along my mate's marred flesh. I was stunned. Their first night of mating and they had claimed each other. I wasn't sure if I was angry or simply jealous.

I sank lower, placing my ass on my heels, and lay my head on Patrick's lap. He stroked his fingers through my hair, soothing me. I needed to ground myself.

It wasn't our time yet. We barely knew each other. Patrick had known Tyler for over twenty years. Their need to mate and claim each other had been simmering for a long time.

"I'm not mad," I said. "A little thrown off, but not mad."

"We'll get there, you and I."

I nodded, comforted by the feel of his warm skin on my cheek. "I know." I wished it would come soon but I sensed Patrick would need to feel at least some level of affection for me before he would respond to me with the necessary ancestral words in a claiming ceremony.

He would need to *feel* something for me.

I was already partway there for him.

Our night together had started my heart beating in the direction of deep devotion. Patrick was sweet and intelligent, and when he spoke of his family, it was with enduring love in his eyes.

I hoped someday, he would look at me like that.

We were fated, so one day we *would* love each other—but how hard?

I wanted the kind of love my brother, Mark, and his mate, Reese, shared.

"Can we go lay down together?" Patrick asked. "I'm exhausted." He used his finger to lift my chin, so I'd look up at him. "And I need you to hold me. I need my fated mate."

That was what I needed as well. To have Patrick curled up against my side, talking in his sleep. He had made me chuckle two nights ago. He'd been having a sleep-induced conversation with himself about getting kittens for the four pups. I wasn't sure if it was something based on reality or if Patrick was simply pondering it over in his mind as he slept.

I'd known very few wolves with cats.

Maybe the four pups *should* have kittens.

I undressed and joined Patrick in bed. He cuddled close to me as I wrapped him up in my arms. I kissed his head. "That's quite the impressive assortment of marks Tyler left on you."

"I think he was trying to send a message."

"And you let him."

Patrick shook as he laughed. "Not going to lie ... kind of liked the method of the message."

I hugged him closer to me. "You're a handful."

"I've been told that."

"I liked the scent of Tyler's seed on you."

"Figured that out." Patrick played his fingers through the hair on my chest. "Did you like the fact there was someone else's seed in me ... or that it was Tyler's?"

"Mm ... definitely Tyler's."

"You're attracted to his scent?"

I furrowed my brow as I chose my words. "I find it pleasant."

Patrick snorted against my side. "Pleasant? You were licking my insides with your tongue."

I shifted my shoulders and exhaled. "Okay, more than pleasant."

"That's going to turn Tyler on."

My pulse flooded my ears and my heart felt as if it tumbled into my stomach. This connection with Tyler just became much more interesting. "Does he like my scent on you?"

Patrick caught my gaze and smiled at me. "Loves it."

My cock stirred as thoughts of Tyler inhaling my scent on Patrick's skin and becoming aroused filled my mind. I wondered if his cock was as beautiful as Patrick's.

Patrick snuck his hand from my chest down to my cock. He made a sound of appreciation when he found it was hard. He kissed my pec and scooted under the blankets.

His mouth on my cock was like heaven.

As we relaxed in the afterglow and Patrick settled in and fell asleep, I set my mind to imagine where I'd be leaving marks for Tyler to find.

TWO WEEKS WENT BY, and Tyler and I had fallen into a routine. Patrick's body was always covered in fresh hickeys. It worked well. The competition between us fired up Patrick's desire.

My time with Patrick, though. It wasn't all about mating. Patrick and I had begun spending more time simply talking, and sharing stories of our lives. Since the spring nights were still cold, we often found ourselves curled up on the sofa in front of the fire, laughing and teasing each other.

Holding one another. Enjoying slow, loving kisses. Caressing and massaging each other without it leading to anything more. There was an ease between us now.

Last night Patrick had told me he was falling in love with me.

I had clung to him so tightly that he had started laughing.

I already loved him.

I hadn't told him yet … but I loved him deeply.

I came home to find Patrick naked in the kitchen, making himself some tea. This was a new thing of his; shedding his clothes as soon as he stepped inside my house.

Living in a compound house with other wolves had restricted his natural inclination to be naked whenever he was indoors. I loved how accessible it made him.

I also loved how beautiful his body was in the glow of the incandescent lights.

Combined with his alluring and joyous personality, he was my perfect mate.

I walked up behind him, wrapped my arms around his waist, and kissed the back of his neck. "Sorry, I'm late tonight. How was your day?"

"Well …." He turned in my arms and held my face. "I had a lot of trouble getting any work done today. I spent most of my day with my head in the toilet at the garage."

My heart thudded and my stomach felt like it flipped.

"You mean …?"

Patrick grinned at me. "Did a pregnancy test a few hours ago. That's a definite *yes*."

I wrapped my arms around him tighter and swung him in circles kissing his face. Patrick was laughing by the time I set him down on his feet.

"Sorry," I said. "That probably didn't help with your nausea."

"Not too bad right now. This morning, though. Sheesh."

"Did Tyler take care of you?"

"He did." Patrick kissed me. "Comforted me in the bathroom. Bought some ginger for tea. Made it for me." He stroked his hand down my cheek. "He left you a special gift."

As soon as I had walked in the door, I detected the scent of Tyler's seed was stronger than usual. I started at Patrick's neck, inhaled, and followed the scent to its source.

I smiled.

Tyler had obviously coated Patrick's stomach in his seed. Power move.

It made my cock hard.

I kneeled at Patrick's feet and dragged my tongue across the skin of his belly. A belly that now contained our pup. I groaned and shut my eyes to savor the strong taste of Tyler's seed.

Patrick's skin was covered in it.

"He dumped his seed on me, had me smear it around, and put my clothes back on."

So cheeky.

Tyler had entirely grown on me.

As I licked Patrick's stomach clean, his muscles jumped and clenched. I swirled my tongue in his belly button. Tyler's seed was thick there.

I kissed his belly and looked up at him as my body surged with need. A desperate need for Patrick. And a mind-altering need for the source of the scent I'd been savoring for weeks.

"I want to meet him."

Patrick tipped his head to one side. "I'll have to ask him if that's all right. Honestly, I'm not sure how he'll feel about meeting you."

"He must be curious about me."

Patrick smiled. "Oh, yeah … he's curious. Sometimes he wants me to describe to him what you do to me … in great detail."

My cock swelled, making my pants extremely uncomfortable. "He does?" It had never occurred to me that

Tyler would be turned on by what Patrick and I did while we were mating.

I rose to my feet, assaulted Patrick's mouth, then turned him to face the counter. I sucked at the back of his ear, breathing heavily into it. "Make sure you tell him about this." I took my cock, slipped it inside him, and grasped both his hips as I drove it home.

Patrick sighed and reached back for my ass with one hand; the other hand bracing himself against the counter. I moved one hand to protect his belly from the hard surface. I stroked my left hand along his throat, stopping just below his jawline. I held him in place.

I was rougher with him than usual.

Patrick spilled first, painting the lower cupboards. I was close behind, jamming into him until he rose on his toes and growled, the vibration of his throat filling my palm.

I thrust into him as my seed filled him.

I turned him to face me after slipping my spent cock from his ass. I held his face in both hands and pressed our foreheads together. He smiled and grasped my wrists.

I loved my mate so much, but this wasn't the time to tell him. I'd acted like a brute, taking him like that in the kitchen. That's *not* how we typically were together. Our mating was usually tender.

"I'm having trouble believing we have a pup coming," I said. "*Our* pup."

Patrick moved closer and draped his arms around my neck. His breath was warm on my ear. "It's a pup borne of love, Declan. I've been thinking about that and you all day."

I smiled. "With your head in the toilet."

Patrick laughed. "Resting my face on the cold porcelain gave me time to think." He stepped back. His eyes were rimmed with tears. "I wasn't sure it would happen when I first met you."

"That we would find love?"

Patrick nodded. "I love Tyler so much; I didn't think there would be room for more love."

"You're no longer falling for me?"

Patrick shook his head, his gaze locked on mine. A tear rolled down his cheek.

"I love you, Declan. With every piece of my heart I have left to give … I love you."

My pulse soared. Those words created a stir in my heart, an intensity of which I hadn't thought was possible. I needed to kiss him. I swooped in and collected his face in both hands.

"I love you too."

Then I sealed my deep devotion with a kiss.

Chapter Eight | Patrick

I was in love with Declan, and we had a pup coming. Somehow, there was room beyond Tyler and our pups in my heart for more love. My family would soon be expanding.

Now for Tyler to finally meet Declan.

Declan was in the shower, getting ready for bed. I lifted the phone receiver and dialed the house I lived in with Tyler. I was hoping for Tyler, but Danny answered the call.

"Hey, congratulations! Tyler tells us you're pregnant," Danny said.

"Yeah, Declan and I are excited." I fiddled with the phone cord. "Is Tyler there?"

"Just saw him heading upstairs. I'll bring him the phone."

Carl, Danny, and the rest of the West Creekside pack had asked very few questions. They knew Tyler and I had claimed each other as mates. And they knew I had a fated mate as well.

Carl, our leader, grunted and shook his head as we explained our situation but hadn't given us any orders to abandon what we were doing. Not that we would have stopped if we'd been told to.

"Hey, Patrick." Tyler's love traveled through the phone line in his voice.

"My beautiful Omega."

"How did it go? Did you tell Declan you're pregnant?"

I smiled. "He's thrilled. Loved your gift too."

Tyler snort-laughed. "Thought I was pushing it."

"In all the right directions, trust me." I rearranged the blanket on my lap. "So …."

"What?"

"Declan wants to meet you."

Silence.

"Not sure how I would handle that," Tyler said at last. "You're having his pup."

"You're going to have to meet him at some point. This pup is going to be part of our family. I'm not keeping them separate. You and our pups will be a part of this pup's life."

"I want that."

"I know you do. So … will you meet him?"

"When?"

"He has business in Creekside tomorrow. Do you mind if he stops by?"

"Tomorrow?"

"If you're not ready, we can arrange another time."

Tyler sighed. "No, tomorrow is fine."

"I'll let him know to come by in the afternoon."

"I'd only do this for you, Patrick. I love you."

"Love you too."

"See you in the morning," Tyler said. "Sleep well, my Omega."

"Good night, my sweet mate."

I hung up the phone and shuffled down into the bedding to wait for Declan. I had no inkling of the unimaginable situation that was about to unfold tomorrow.

Chapter Nine | Tyler

I'm not sure why I was so nervous. I felt like I knew Declan already. Patrick had told me everything about him. And the taste of the seed Declan had painted Patrick's belly with as a response to my bold move yesterday was still fresh on my tongue and lips.

I liked it when Declan's scent lingered on me.

Logan had started the morning playfully harassing us. To any wolf sensibilities, including his because he was trapped in the garage with us, we reeked.

I'd mated with Patrick in the office before we'd opened the service bays for business. His hole had still been wet with Declan's seed. We'd knocked everything off the desk so I could fill him with *my* seed, clean his belly with my tongue, and coax him to coat my throat.

Then we'd taken a moment to hold each other and kiss, reconnecting.

God, I loved him.

A big, fancy car pulled up outside the bay doors. It had to be Declan. It was only 12:15. Slim definition of the afternoon. I counted that as a strike against him.

His driver's door swung open, and I had to cling to the workbench.

The scent I'd become addicted to wafted past me.

Declan came around the car and stood near the hood, staring at me.

Shit.

I swallowed.

He was gorgeous. Patrick hadn't done his looks justice. Declan was a tall wolf with broad shoulders that filled out an expensive-looking grey suit. A white shirt and tie created a cradle for his sensual face with high cheekbones. Brown hair with gold flecks, and eyes to match.

I licked my lips.

His were so incredibly kissable.

He adjusted his cuffs and tie. His silver cufflinks glimmered in the sunlight. He was pure sophistication. I took a few plodding steps toward the door of the bay, inhaling.

I felt as if I was being pulled by a magnet.

I was aware that my mouth was hanging open, but I couldn't close it.

"Tyler," Declan said as he walked toward me; his low rumbling voice making me tremble. Patrick stepped back, allowing Declan to approach me unhindered. There was no need for formal introductions. I knew everything I needed to know about Declan.

He wasn't my fated mate, but he was the damned closest thing to it. I nearly crumpled to my knees as Declan stood before me and cradled my face in one hand.

He said my name again.

I whimpered as I nestled my cheek into his touch and brushed it up and down his palm until he used his thumb to stroke my skin. I glanced at Patrick. He was barely breathing.

I flicked my gaze back to Declan and didn't stray from his attention again.

I heard Logan whisper, "Jeezus," as Declan hovered over me and kissed me with the most seductive lips I'd ever experienced. I had to cling to him to maintain my balance.

His hands moved to my hips.

I was surprised when an extra hand touched my shoulder.

Declan broke from our kiss and lifted his hand to cradle Patrick's face which had appeared beside ours. I shuddered through a shallow ecstatic breath as Declan took Patrick's mouth.

The sounds of their exhalations and desire reached my cock.

Then Declan was back on my lips.

I was hungrier for him this time. Now that I knew Patrick was into it. That our kissing was turning Patrick on. There was a three-way scent of desire emanating from our bodies.

Declan bit my bottom lip, holding it in his teeth as he released my mouth. The vice grip pinched as he pulled until it broke free. He walked backward not breaking eye contact with us, holding one each of our hands, and pulled us along with him. The progress was like slow motion. His steps toward his car were measured and deliberate.

I think he was trying not to scare me.

He opened the back door and held it open. Patrick was the first to enter. I slipped in behind him. Declan followed us both and closed the door. The interior was almost entirely black. The only light was coming from the front windshield and the passenger windows.

"Kiss for me," Declan said.

My cock pulsed. I wasn't sure how I had ended up here, but a wave of rippling lust washed over me. Patrick gripped my chin and brought our lips together. I sank into the familiarity of them. I moaned and thrust my tongue deeper when Declan's hand came to rest on the back of my neck.

The pressure of his hand was authoritative but not aggressive.

Patrick's hand drifted from my chin, down my chest, to my cock. He caressed it through my coveralls until my mind became focused on him. Then Declan's hand started to pull my arm from my sleeve. My attention snapped back to him, rapt. He wanted me to undress.

He peeled Patrick's coveralls off his shoulder.

Declan sat closer to the door as Patrick and I struggled out of our clothes. Declan gathered everything up and tossed our stuff onto the front passenger seat.

He brushed his hands down our bare chests.

"Beautiful," he whispered.

His palms traveled down our chests to our hard cocks. Patrick and I both groaned and widened our legs as much as we could as he wrapped his fist around our shafts and stroked us slowly.

Patrick placed his hand on my inner thigh. I turned my face and captured his lips which were poised above my shoulder. Our hands dug into each other's hair, clinging to clumps.

"Fill him," Declan said, his voice thick with desire. His hand wandered from my cock to my chin to break my lips' contact with Patrick to look at him. "I want to see you fill him."

My cock pulsed at the suggestion of having Declan watch us. Patrick decided on the position. There wasn't much room, but he managed to straddle my lap, his hands on my shoulders.

I couldn't believe we were doing this—but I couldn't stop myself.

Patrick rose on his knees, I held my cock, and he descended on it. He tossed his head back and dug his nails into my shoulders as he came to rest on my lap, his cock pressed to my stomach.

He placed one hand on the ceiling, an easy rise and fall, while I gripped his ass to guide him.

I peered over at Declan, needing to know if we were pleasing him. He stroked the front of his pants as he watched us. His gaze was hungry but calm.

Patrick grunted, bouncing faster on my cock. I returned my attention to him. He held my face and kissed me, his tongue wild with desire. Declan's hand slipped between us. His fist bumped against my abs as he pumped Patrick's cock. Patrick's channel clenched around my girth.

It was pure bliss as he howled, filled the cab with sound, and spilled his seed. The scent of it combined with the scent of Declan's arousal in the small space had my balls lifting.

Declan raised his fingers to my mouth, feeding me what Patrick had released. I chased his fingers and groaned as Declan retreated with them and kept them for himself.

I planted my feet on the floor of the car, held Patrick in place with my hands on his hips, and hammered my cock into him. Declan stuck his thumb in my mouth and pried my jaw open by hooking onto my teeth. His control of me awoke a submissive need I didn't know I possessed.

I cried out, gurgling, and filled my mate with my seed.

Declan wasn't done with us yet. He brushed his fingers along Patrick's ass. "I want some." I shivered. His finger stroked my balls and touched my shaft and Patrick's hole.

Patrick rose away from me, slipping my cock from his ass.

"Yes, Alpha," he said.

Declan leaned closer to Patrick, his arm pumping up and down. When he was satisfied, Declan brought his hand around and used his damp finger to draw a circle on my nipple.

My heart skipped a new rhythm of beats.

I groaned, clenched Declan's arm, and tipped my head back as Declan took my fragrant nipple into his mouth and sucked on it. I could have seeded Patrick again if my cock had recovered.

We were all silent as Declan retreated and Patrick sat back beside me.

Instead of collecting our clothes and giving them back to us, Declan climbed out of the car, reappeared in the driver's seat, and started the car.

I settled into the seat as Declan pulled out onto the road.

Nude and kidnapped was a distinct possibility.

AN HOUR LATER, we pulled up outside a large log home. It was the imposing house of a pack leader. Riverton. Declan had taken us to his home.

We didn't receive our clothes back.

It had snowed this far up in the mountains. After Declan opened the back door of the car, Patrick and I dashed naked the distance from the car to the steps in our bare feet.

The blast of warm air as we walked in through the front door was welcome.

Declan swung the door closed. "Kiss for me again."

This time, Patrick and I were able to bring our nude bodies together fully. I wrapped my arms around his chest with his draped over my shoulders, his fingers in my hair.

The kiss was sweet and slow, reassuring one another.

We both wanted this.

"Up to the bedroom," Declan said. "Lean over on the foot of the bed."

Patrick linked his fingers with mine as we walked up the stairs. We kept holding hands as we lay our chests on the foot of the bed, asses in the air, legs parted slightly, our hips touching.

I turned my head so I could see Patrick's face.

He smiled at me and mouthed, "I love you."

I returned the sentiment without speaking aloud.

I broke contact with Patrick's gaze, groaned, and closed my eyes as Declan's hand stroked my ass and gave it a quick slap. He pushed a finger into my hole and pumped it a few times.

He extracted it and I could hear him inhaling deeply.

"You're in heat," he said to me.

"I am. Two days now."

Declan grunted and lined his cock up with my hole. My stomach felt squirrely. My cock jumped against the bedding. He was going to mate with me, knowing he might put a pup in me.

I felt weak, my need to feel his cock inside me, plundering my insides, strong.

Unstoppable.

"Please, Alpha," I whined.

He gripped my hips and slipped into me. My eyes nearly rolled back in my head as my tight ring burned. It had been years since anyone had filled my hole.

Declan's hands caressed my ass and gave it another slap as he pounded into me.

I whimpered when he withdrew.

Patrick groaned beside me. He held tighter to my hand as he was jostled up and back on the bed, his chest rubbing the bedding. I heard Declan smack his ass.

Declan's hands moved back to my ass, and he drove his cock into me. This time it was me being jostled. His thrusts were aggressive, bordering on frenzied—but rhythmic.

He switched back to Patrick. I could sense the tension rising in Declan. The sound of his grunts and groans changed. He was close to climaxing.

I trembled as Declan drove back into my hole. He was choosing me to be filled with his seed. I whimpered as he roared and thrust hard into me and held it there.

A few more high slow penetrations and I knew he had seeded me.

He squeezed my ass and patted it. "Scoot up the bed."

The message was meant for both of us because Patrick crawled up the bed alongside me. Declan came up the bed. He had undressed while we'd been waiting for him at the end of the bed.

He lay between us and gathered us in his arms. Both Patrick and I placed our heads on his bare shoulders and tucked our faces against the sides of his neck.

"Such sweet Omegas," Declan said and kissed each of our foreheads. He gave Patrick an extra kiss and tugged him closer. "I love you."

"I love you too, Alpha." Patrick raked his fingers through the abundant hair on Declan's chest. I felt left out even though Declan had chosen to fill me with his seed.

My urge was to mate with him again.

I couldn't blame it all on being in heat. I kissed Declan's cheek, making him hum. My stomach churned with excitement at his sound of approval. I desperately wanted to please him.

It had built slowly over weeks, but in some way, our connection felt fated.

He whispered something to Patrick.

Patrick smiled and nodded.

My mate climbed over Declan and shoved my legs apart. He made himself comfortable between them and took my cock into his mouth. He played with my balls as he sucked.

Declan gripped my face, turned it to him, and kissed me. A possessive, all-consuming kiss. I melted into it, giving him everything. He released my mouth and held my chin.

"We'll spend some time together just you and I—talking. I want to get to know you better." He touched my left pec. "What's inside here." He nuzzled my hair. "Our connection feels fated."

"Yes ...." It's all I could manage. Declan's words had overwhelmed me, and Patrick's mouth was close to drawing the seed from my body. I wasn't sure which was more distracting.

Declan closed his mouth over mine again. This time more loving.

My heart skipped a beat.

It was excited to immerse myself in more time with him.

Chapter Ten | Declan

I played over in my mind our first time when we were all together as I sat in the back booth at *Growlers*. The three of us had spent until late evening mating. I'd paid special attention to Tyler.

He needed to know I cared for him.

I'd spoken the truth to Tyler that night. I felt as if we were fated in our own way. It wasn't the same strength of pull I'd felt toward Patrick, but it was close. All those nights inhaling the scent of his seed had nearly driven me insane. I had wanted to experience its presence firsthand.

Now I had … and it was glorious.

Tyler and I had met up twice this past week. Both times at *Growlers*. I wanted to take mating off the table. These meetings were about getting to know each other better.

Today, I had some more personal questions beyond his childhood, his love of being a mechanic, and his obsession with motorbikes. I brightened as he walked toward me.

Tyler was beautiful—an angelic rebel.

He slid into the booth and smiled at me.

In addition to meeting with me to talk, Patrick, Tyler, and I had continued mating nightly. We'd been meeting for over a week. Today, Tyler phoned me to tell me he felt sick.

I reached for his hand, and he took mine.

"Tell me what's going on," I said.

Tyler shook his head. "Not sure yet, but it's possible I'm with pup."

I squeezed his hand. "And how do you feel about that?"

Tyler sucked on his bottom lip. "That depends. I don't want to raise a pup alone."

I leaned closer to the table. "That would never happen, Tyler." I set my other hand on our joined hands. "We're as close to being fated mates as two wolves could ever be, you and I."

I could see Tyler relax his shoulders.

He nodded but didn't speak.

"You're still concerned," I said.

Tyler sighed and pulled his hand away. "We haven't howled a song together yet."

We hadn't. I had hoped to find time with Tyler alone to sing a song together. Now, that he was likely pregnant by me, I could see why he was worried about my commitment.

"Let's go back to my house."

Tyler frowned. "I can't leave work right now."

"Then come tonight—just you." I caught his gaze and held it. I wanted him to know how important this was to me. "I'll speak to Patrick. Let him know we need time alone."

Tyler shifted in his seat.

"I can tell him. He's been asking how it's going between us. Especially, this morning, now that I'm not feeling good. It's no secret that he wants everything to work out between us all."

"And that's what you want as well?"

This time Tyler reached for my hand. "Declan … of course."

I folded my fingers against his palm. I needed the reassurance of his words and touch. It didn't happen often enough. There were things the three of us didn't discuss yet. Time talking was becoming easier when we weren't all mating. It was a strange dynamic to get used to. Sometimes, I missed my time alone with Patrick. I knew that would come back.

Right now, the three of us were practically obsessed with each other and the newness of our situation.

Patrick and I still found time to speak words of love and connection.

Our words always lit up a brightness in Tyler's eyes.

I relished the times when Patrick and Tyler shared loving words with one another.

Now, we were potentially expecting two pups.

The three of us *did* need to talk together. In the next couple of days, Tyler would know for sure if he was pregnant. A discussion needed to happen about my Omegas moving in with me.

Patrick had expressed that he was worried about their business and his accessibility to their four pups. It was only an hour's commute, so it wasn't unreasonable to maintain both.

Tyler needed to be included in the conversation.

"I need to get back to work," Tyler said and smiled. "I'll phone you if I start puking."

I laughed. "Much appreciated."

We rose from our seats and Tyler folded himself into my embrace. I kissed him on the head, then Tyler looked up at me and I kissed him. I cradled him, my lips on his until he hummed with contentment. My heart pattered a little harder and faster.

He felt good in my arms.

I had fallen hard for him.

"Love you," I whispered against his lips—courage finally winning out.

Tyler clung tighter to me and buried his face against my shoulder. When he pulled away, his face was a mess of tears. He smiled at me. "I want to be yours, my loving Alpha."

The claiming ceremony. We really did have a lot to discuss—the three of us. Patrick and I hadn't even claimed each other yet. Tyler had come on the scene before we had a chance.

Plus, there was how Patrick felt about Tyler. The strength of their love.

Recently, it hadn't felt like the right time.

"Are you sure that's what you want?" I asked.

Tyler looked around at the crowded restaurant. "We can talk later—when we're alone."

I nodded. "Of course. Give me a call when you're leaving, and I'll head home."

Tyler winked at me as he backed away from me, then turned and jogged out the door.

I groaned.

Yeah, totally in love with him.

I STOKED THE FIRE in the fireplace. Tyler had called me to say he was leaving the garage. He'd be here any minute. I lit a few candles and piled a stack of blankets on the sofa.

I looked around the vast living room. It felt comfy. The amber logs reflected the warm color of the flames. The air was fragrant. I had a pot of ginger tea simmering on the stove.

The *puking* had started.

The front door popped open and shut. A gust of cold air made its way to the living room. I could hear Tyler rustling around in the front entry, storing his coat and boots.

"Is that ginger tea I smell?" he called, his voice carrying from the direction of the kitchen.

"Do you want me to get it for you?"

"No … I'm good."

From the area of the stove, the clatter of the ladle against the metal pot, and the *tink* sound of it touching a ceramic mug.

The sputtering sound of the honey. More *tinks* as he stirred the tea.

I couldn't contain a smile as Tyler wandered into the living room. I had started imagining his belly swollen with our pup. Patrick's was already round and soft beneath my lips.

"Sit with me," I said, patting the sofa cushion beside me. Once Tyler was settled, sitting leaned on one hip with his arm on the armrest, and his feet on the sofa, I wrapped a blanket around his feet and massaged them. He deserved every attention I could shower on him.

Tyler groaned and wiggled his toes. "That feels so good. Been on my feet all day." He smiled at me. "Except for when I was on my knees in front of that damned toilet."

"Not the first time."

"No, the triplets had me throwing up for weeks."

"How was your pregnancy with them?"

"Hard. I should have stopped working. Patrick wanted me to. He insisted I only do simple jobs. My back was killing me most of the time. He was probably right. I should have rested."

"Patrick told me you both cared for the triplets for the first two months."

"We did. Until Harlan and Logan's pup was 6 weeks old."

"Those two months must have brought you two closer together."

Tyler nodded. "That's when I knew for sure, I was in love with Patrick."

"He was in love with you for much longer than that."

"Apparently. Wish he'd said something." Tyler blew on his tea and took a sip.

"Would that have made a difference?"

"I might have examined my feelings for him more closely."

"Over twenty years of living and working together is a long time to not know."

Tyler set his tea on the coffee table and looked at me. "I want to talk about you and me."

Okay. Touchy subject.

I squeezed his foot. "You said today that you want to be mine."

"I do." He set his hand on mine. "You said today that you love me."

"I do."

Tyler covered his mouth and lifted his other hand. "Just a sec. I should be all right for the night, but you never know. I had some nighttime bouts of nausea with the triplets."

I rubbed Tyler's back as he composed himself.

He lifted the cup back to his lips and inhaled the scent of it.

"You all right?" I asked.

"Feeling a little sweaty but it'll pass."

"Can I get you anything else?"

"Do you have any eggs? Sometimes they help."

I hastily found my feet and headed for the kitchen. "Chicken or quail?"

"Quail if you have them. Cracked in a glass. The shells gross me out."

Noted.

I cracked six quail eggs in a glass tumbler, swearing beneath my breath, my thick fingers making a mess of it. I had to fish tiny shards of shells out of the glass with a fork.

It was worth the effort.

Tyler sighed and beamed a smile at me. "Thank you, Alpha."

He swallowed them in one go. I watched him in case I had missed any shells. I wanted everything to be perfect tonight. I didn't want to screw up so early in the night.

I had hopes that he would stay overnight with me.

We needed some alone time.

Even if we just held each other as we fell asleep.

"I want to be yours too," I said, reopening the conversation as I turned on the sofa to face him.

"As claimed mates, right?"

"Tyler, I meant what I said … I'm in love with you."

"You love Patrick, and you haven't claimed him yet."

"We haven't claimed *each other*. It felt like something was missing. I know Patrick felt it. I never started the ceremony because I sensed he might back away. His love for you is intense."

Tyler sighed. "When Patrick and I claimed each other, I never thought I would be claimed by another. I knew Patrick and you would find your way to each other—you're fated. But me?"

There was only one thing I could think of doing to prove myself. I slipped off the sofa and kneeled in front of Tyler. I took both his hands in mine and stared intently into his eyes.

It was a human custom … but I didn't care.

He needed to know how much I loved him.

"Tyler Carmichael, would you do me the honor of becoming my committed fated mate?"

Tyler blinked at me a few times and swallowed.

Tears rimmed his eyes.

He nodded as he snuffled, then reached for my face. "Kiss me, you lovesick Alpha." His lips were tender and wet, and he tasted of eggs and ginger, reminding me he was pregnant.

With *our* pup.

It wasn't often I cried, but the momentous reminder brought tears to my eyes.

Tyler pulled back, still holding my face. "In case you missed it … that's a *yes*."

I laughed. "Yeah, I figured that out."

Tyler sighed. "You've made the living room look lovely, but can we go to bed now?"

I rose from my knees, took his hand, and led him to the bedroom. As I looked down at him beneath me in bed, filling him, his mouth open, his lashes fluttering, I felt complete.

Patrick and Tyler.

My Omegas.

Tyler and I opened our throats and sang a song of devotion.

I loved them both to the depth of my soul.

Chapter Eleven | Patrick

Tyler and I held hands as we drove to Declan's. He was 3 weeks pregnant now and I was in my fifth week. My belly was round and firm, and the pup had started moving around.

My beloved mate had spent a lot of time with his lips to my stomach, speaking and singing to our little unborn pup. It would know Tyler's voice and that filled me with joy.

We released our grip on each other as we turned off onto the Riverton compound driveway. I needed both hands on the wheel. It was bumpy and needed a new layer of gravel that Declan had committed to spreading in the summer. I pulled up outside Declan's house.

"I think I know where tonight's conversation is going," I said.

"Me too." Tyler opened his door. "It's time."

"I suppose." I was going to miss the odd nights when Tyler and I stayed overnight at Danny's house. The same house we had been living together in for over twenty years.

We had pushed two of the twin beds together so we could curl up in each other's arms to sleep. It was becoming harder to do because of our expanding bellies.

Making love just the two of us had at times become comical. Adam had told me I was big for 5 weeks. Finding my cock beneath my swollen belly had turned into a game where I usually ended up on my back with my legs in the air so Tyler could access my cock and my hole with his mouth.

It would do my back in typically. And the only way Tyler could penetrate me is if I was on my hands and knees, his growing belly thumping against my ass.

Those nights alone with Tyler were numbered.

Tonight, Declan would be asking us to move in with him.

It made sense. We were about to become a family of five. Our pups needed a stable home life. Not one where they were being dragged back and forth between homes.

The uncomfortable part for me was leaving our pack. It was the pack of my birth. I had imagined myself living among them until I was old, surrounded by members on my deathbed.

Tyler by my side.

I was convinced we would go into the afterlife together.

I followed Tyler into the house where Declan was waiting for us. He was preparing food in the kitchen. Mountains of cubed venison. Tyler and I always tended to be famished.

Declan rushed to us.

"You made good time." He cradled my face and kissed me, then did the same with Tyler. I smiled. Declan was acting giddy, grinning, then bounced back over to the counter.

It settled my uncomfortable feelings. I was in love with Declan. I was in love with Tyler. Living together with both was going to be incredible. We just needed to work out some details.

"Come. Sit." Declan brought the food into the dining room. The table was set up with candles, the good plates, and a bottle of non-alcoholic champagne. He'd gone all out. The attention to detail reminded me what a sweet and caring wolf he was. He was going to make a fantastic sire.

Tyler and I took seats to his left and his right. As Alpha, he sat at the head of the table. Despite his commitment to modernizing his pack, he still displayed a lot of traditional views.

An exception since we were pregnant was he encouraged us to feed at the same time as him. Not sure if that would last once the pups were born, but for now, it showed his desire to change.

He poured us each a glass of the bubbly pup-safe wine, then raised his glass, and Tyler and I brought ours to his, clinking them. This would be a night of celebration.

After we drank, I filled my plate, saw red, and tore into my meal.

The snarls and growls as my two mates did the same made me feel at home.

Declan handed me a rolled wet and warm cloth to clean myself with after I finished feeding. I burped as I cleaned my hands, hoping tonight wouldn't find me with heartburn again.

"We need to have a conversation," Declan started.

"About our living arrangement," Tyler replied.

"Yes." Declan took our plates and stacked them on his. "It doesn't make sense for you to keep your room over in West Creekside territory."

"There *are* wolves who could use it," I said. "What about our business?"

"I think you should keep it," Declan replied. "You both love what you do, and Riverton already has a full-service garage. As leader, I couldn't allow you to set up another."

"I don't think we'd have any trouble selling the business," Tyler said. "It's not something I want to do, though. We've been running that business since we were twenty. It's our life."

"The pups are going to be our life," I said. "What happens with them?"

"My Beta is more than willing to watch them during the day," Declan said. "Could Logan manage the business for two months until the pups are weaned?"

I made a tsking sound. "He doesn't know much about cars."

"What about Carl's eldest pup?" Tyler said. "He's nineteen. I always see him working on cars."

I nodded. "We could get Logan to run the business end of things. Poke our heads in occasionally. Make sure the books and the inventory for the store are being maintained properly. He should be able to manage the shop end of things. He's been with us for over 6 years."

"Then it's settled," Declan said. "You'll both move in?"

Tyler reached for and took Declan's hand. I set my hand in Declan's other hand and lay my hand, palm up, on the table for Tyler to take. Our joined hands formed a perfect triangle.

"We're in this together," I said. "We're mates—the three of us."

I'd never seen Declan look so happy.

"I love you both," he said. "As your Alpha, I vow to protect you."

I smirked. So old-fashioned, but I appreciated the sentiment. The world was a dangerous place for our species. We were outnumbered in the extreme by humans. Our existence was simply tolerated by many. Having someone as powerful as our Alpha as a protector brought me peace.

He would fight anyone to the death to keep us and our pups safe.

"When do you want us to move in?" I asked as we released our hands.

"Tomorrow?" Declan replied.

"Wow," Tyler said. "That's quick. Not that we have a lot of stuff."

I laughed. "Your clothes alone are going to take an entire trip."

"Feeling attacked." Tyler smiled at me. "But you're right."

"I had more than a housing conversation planned for tonight," Declan said, his brow dipping. He looked nervous. He folded his hands together on the table. "A couple of weeks ago, I proposed to Tyler, asking him to be my committed fated mate and he agreed to do me the honor."

I knew this already. Tyler had told me.

"And Patrick …." Declan's gaze landed on me. "Fate has chosen you as my fated mate. And I couldn't be more thrilled. My love for you started from that fate but has grown exponentially."

He looked at Tyler. "And I love you too … so much."

"You want us all to be committed," I guessed. "To perform the ceremony."

"We're complete," Declan replied. "I think it's time."

Tyler pushed his seat back and rose to his feet. "Where? When?"

"Now and I think the shower would be best," Declan said. "There's going to be a lot of blood."

Discussing it was taking the romance out of it. I joined Tyler on my feet. He was thinking the same thing as me. I approached Tyler at his corner of the table. He was ready for me.

Tyler took my face in his hands and kissed me, first soft … then desperately. We moaned and grappled with each other's clothing. He had my shirt off first and caressed my softening pecs.

I trembled as he ran his thumb over my puffy nipple.

Declan put his hand on my back. I pulled Tyler's shirt off over his head and tossed it to one side. Our bellies pressed together as we deepened our kiss. Tyler moved his hands to my ass.

Declan grabbed my pants from behind. They had an elastic waistband, so they were easy to pull down. My ass bare, Tyler moved his hands so Declan could kiss one cheek.

Declan stood behind me and sucked on the back of my neck.

I tipped my head to one side, moaning at the possessiveness of his touch. I was his. His and Tyler's. I'd never wanted something more in my life. I unlatched and unzipped Tyler's maternity jeans. He shuffled them off his legs along with his underwear. I grasped his hard cock.

Declan pulled on my hips, encouraging me to follow him.

I released Tyler and we made our way to the ensuite bathroom. Declan started the shower and undressed. Tyler and I entered the shower first, stepping under the hot water. Our cocks prodded at our bellies as we returned to the desire of our lips. Declan ran his hand down my back. I knew he was doing the same to Tyler's. He loved seeing us together, pleasuring one another.

Declan stepped into the shower, turned my face to him, and took my lips. His mouth was tender. He turned to Tyler and kissed him, then brought Tyler and my lips together.

Water ran into our mouths as we devoured and chased our kiss of commitment. Declan placed his hand on the back of my head, pressing Tyler and me closer together.

"I want to be both of yours," he said. "How do I choose who to bite first?"

Tyler stepped back and ran his hand over his wet hair. "Patrick. You fell in love first."

I clung to Tyler's fingers as Declan backed me up against the wall of the shower. He nuzzled my claiming area. "I want to be yours," he whispered in my ear.

"And I yours." I clung to Declan's shoulder and prepared myself. I cried out as Declan's impressive canines pierced my skin. Tyler clung tighter to my hand. A glimmer of joined consciousness pushed on the edge of my mind as Declan sucked on me.

I could sense shades of him.

I whimpered as he released me and turned to Tyler. He was going to claim each of us first. Declan growled as he shoved Tyler to the wall. He was seeing red. I put my hand on Declan's back to calm him. It appeared to work because he slowed his movements and kissed Tyler on the lips before brushing his canines along Tyler's neck to his claiming area.

"I want to be yours," I heard him say to Tyler.

"And I yours," Tyler replied. He clung so hard to my hand that I thought his fingernails were going to leave a mark. Declan bit into him and Tyler was more stoic about it, only whining.

Declan backed himself against the edge of the shower and took our hands. Blood was running in rivulets down from Tyler's claiming area across his collarbone and down his chest.

Declan gathered us in his arms.

"We want you to be ours," I said.

Declan licked his lips. "And I yours … both."

He held us as we moved to the claiming areas on either side of his neck. I was still nuzzling Declan's flesh when Tyler bit him. The urge washed over me, and I sunk my canines into Declan.

We both sucked on him.

The consciousness link opened with a snap, and I was flooded with images of how much Declan and Tyler loved each other. Tyler hadn't told Declan he loved him yet.

Now, it was evident to everyone.

We released Declan and the three of us launched into howling the song of commitment. It echoed in the shower stall and was soon joined by the rest of the Riverton pack.

Declan hugged us tight to him.

I suspected all three of us were crying. Our bodies were certainly trembling.

The mating that followed took on more significance.

The three of us had become one.

I CHASED ROSE down the hallway of Harlan and Logan's house. She had taken off with one of Reese's dinosaurs. Reese was bawling his eyes out. Rose was shrieking with delight.

The fact I was 8 weeks pregnant didn't help things. Our pup would be coming any day now. Both Tyler and I were suffering. He was only two weeks behind me.

Declan had his hands full giving us nightly foot rubs.

"Rose!" Tyler shouted. "Stop!"

I smirked. My mate was extra grumpy today. He loved watching the pups for Harlan and Logan, but his back was bothering him. He was chewing his way through bags of willow bark.

The healer had warned him to slow down.

Hence, the grumpiness.

He was in pain.

I caught Rose by one arm as she completed the house's circuit. I held out my other hand. "Give me the dinosaur." She pouted at me but handed it over. "Now let's go apologize to Reese."

"Do I have to? Why don't you make him share?"

"He made a pile of dinosaurs for you to play with. You took off with one that wasn't in your pile." I held up the dinosaur. Some kind of tyrannosaurus. "You know this one is his favorite."

"I like it too."

Tyler wandered into the hallway with us. "No, you don't. Play with the wooden trains Uncle Patrick bought for you. I'll help you make some blanket forts for them to drive through."

I brushed my hand down Tyler's arm. "You going to be okay doing that?"

"I'm already in agony. What's the difference?"

"Stop." I shoved him. "Go sit. I'll throw a few blankets over chairs."

Tyler held my face and kissed me. "Thank you."

Rose hauled on my hand. "Come on, Uncle. I know what blankets to use."

For the next twenty minutes, I draped blankets in the family room over the backs of dining room chairs and shuffled them apart to make sure there was enough room for the rambunctious onslaught of little wolves racing through the *tunnels* before they were even complete.

Tyler waddled into the family room, sat on the sofa, and put his feet on the coffee table. The living room hadn't been hectic enough for him. He liked to be near the pups.

I plopped down beside him.

An ache surged from my hole up through my channel. Tyler had told me that meant I was close. That whelping could be as soon as hours away.

Tyler placed his hand on my stomach and rubbed small circles on it.

"No contractions yet?" he asked.

"Just yesterday for a few minutes." I wiggled my ass into the sofa cushion to relieve the pressure on my sore hips. I splayed my legs, lay my head back on the backrest, and sighed.

That was about as comfortable as I was going to get.

I moved Tyler's hand to the bottom of my belly. The pup had squirmed. Tyler loved to feel it. Soon we would be able to feel his pup moving. He leaned his head on my shoulder.

"I love you," he said.

"You're my forever wolf, my Omega. Love you too."

It had been an incredible experience being pregnant at the same time. When Tyler had been pregnant with the triplets, I had felt left out. That I hadn't given him those pups.

It had hurt.

Now, someone who loved both of us had given us pups.

Elated wasn't a strong enough word.

"Are you going to whelp in the guest room?" Tyler asked.

"Not sure I'll feel comfortable in there."

Tyler kissed my shoulder. "You've already created quite the nest in there."

"I want options."

"I'll be right there with you. So will Declan." I could feel Tyler grin against my shoulder. "Plus, a few Riverton Omegas we don't know very well."

"Ugh. I need to speak to Declan about that. I only need a healer." Harry leaped at my lap, causing me to protect my belly. "Harry, be careful. There's a little pup in here. You know that."

"When is it coming out?"

"Soon," Tyler said.

"I want to play with it."

"It'll be a couple of months until the pup is ready to play." I covered my chest. Talk of the pup had started my nipples leaking. I was wearing pads, but the sensation felt heavy and strange.

Harry climbed off the sofa and went back to crawling through the tunnels.

"Let down?" Tyler guessed.

"My nipples are tingling so much, they feel itchy."

Tyler nudged me. "We'll take care of that for you tonight."

My cock pulsed. "Yes, please." Playtime with the three of us had changed with Tyler and I both being heavily pregnant. Declan was extra attentive, and positions had to be improvised.

Tyler and I exhaled a sigh of relief when we heard Harlan and Logan call out to us from the front hall. A bittersweet sound. We were exhausted and wanted to go home, but this might be the last time we watched the pups for a while. Our hands were about to become very full.

"Did everyone behave?" Harlan asked as he entered the family room. He grinned at us after surveying the room. "Oh, goody. Blanket forts and tunnels to dismantle tonight."

"Maybe we can take advantage of a fort after the pups are in bed before we take them down," Logan said. "Bring back memories of our camping trip together all those years ago."

"Mm." Harlan gathered Logan in his arms and kissed his cheek. "Our first time."

Tyler snorted. "With that, we're going to head out."

Logan peered through one of the tunnels. "Harry, Rose ... Haley, and Reese. Can you come out of there, please? Papa Tyler and Uncle Patrick are leaving."

Haley skidded to a stop in front of us. The others joined her.

"Now, remember what we told you," Harlan said. "They have pups coming. You're not going to see them for a few weeks. And then you'll get to meet their pups."

"Will they be furry like dog puppies?" Rose asked.

"Yes," Tyler replied. "For the first five years, they'll be chaotic furry bundles chasing you around once they're two months old. We'll bring them by once they open their eyes so you can meet them. For the first month, no playing with them other than petting them, though."

Reese clapped his hands together. "I can't wait. We can throw sticks for them."

I laughed. It would be a couple of months more until they'd be interested in chasing sticks. Wrestling, gnawing on things, and nipping at each other would be their main activities until then.

"Let's start with tugging toys and go from there," Harlan said.

"Which reminds me," Logan said. "We have something for you in the front hall."

Each pup received a kiss on the cheek and a hug from both of us before we joined Harlan and Logan by the front door. I had my arm wrapped around Tyler as he sobbed against me.

This was going to be hard on him being away from the pups.

Hard on both of us.

But hardest on Tyler. He had whelped three of those pups.

Logan held up a pup bed designed for newly whelped pups to snuggle into. Our pups would only be two weeks apart. They could share one bed. It was cheery colors; quilted.

We already had one at home, but this one was cuter.

"This is perfect," I said and accepted the gift. Tyler was the first to hug Logan.

"Thank you," he said. "It really is perfect."

I hugged Logan while Tyler had Harlan in his arms. They truly were our best friends. All our other friends were simply acquaintances. Mostly our old housemates.

They weren't part of our pack anymore, though. Our allegiances were toward Riverton pack first and East Creekside pack next where our pups lived.

When we arrived home, Declan ran a hot bath for us in the massive tub in the ensuite bathroom. It was big enough for all three of us, but he'd drawn this bath for Tyler and me.

Declan lit candles, set them around the outside ledge of the tub and on the counter, and dressed the bath water with scented oils. It felt *so* good to slip beneath the water.

Tyler and I faced each other in the tub. We each grabbed a foot of the other and started massaging. Declan left us alone to enjoy each other's company.

What Tyler and I had was beyond special.

I loved Declan but Tyler felt like the mate to my wolf's soul.

Soon we'd be joining each other in the incredible adventure of raising our pups together.

In love.

Forever in love.

Chapter Twelve | Tyler

The bathwater was cooling, and my back, pressed against the hard tub, was killing me. It was time to get out and lay down for a nap. I knew Patrick would agree.

The pups had worn us out.

"Let's get out," I said and fished around for the bathtub plug. I found it and pulled it free so the water would drain. I was the first to stand. Patrick had to struggle to his feet.

I stepped out of the tub and held out both hands for Patrick to take. He clasped them and was slow and careful as he stepped over the edge of the tub and onto the floor.

I took a towel and started with his shoulders, drying him. Down and under his arms, and across his chest. I spent extra time on his belly. The bath oil had slicked it up. After I finished drying him, I pumped some moisturizer into my hand and rubbed it on his stretched skin.

Patrick ran his fingers through my hair. "Thank you."

"I owe you for being so attentive while I was pregnant with the triplets."

"I loved spoiling you. I loved you so much."

I stepped closer, licked my lips, and brought them close to Patrick's.

"I wish I'd known." I pressed a quick kiss to his lips. "I wasn't sure my love for you would be accepted. We'd been close for so long; it was hard to tell if we were still just friends or in love."

Patrick stroked my cheek. "In some way, I've loved you since we met."

I couldn't stop the tears that collected in my eyes. We couldn't dwell on the past. Even though we hadn't been *together*, we had actively loved each other for all those years.

Without me knowing it, my heart had always been Patrick's.

"Towel off," Patrick said. "I need to lie down. I'm sure you do too."

Patrick left me in the bathroom to dry myself. When I entered the bedroom, Patrick was lying on the bed on his side, his belly protruding. His eyes watching me.

God, I loved him.

I climbed onto the bed behind him, leaned over him, and kissed him. He rolled onto his back to seal and deepen our kiss. I brushed my hand down his throat to his chest and cupped his pec.

I thumbed his nipple. It was wet. I pinched it softly until Patrick moaned. The pressure and release of milk would help relieve some of the itchy feeling. I moved over to the other nipple.

With my wet fingers, I caressed Patrick's belly. The milk combined with the bath oil made a slippery surface. Over the mound of his swollen stomach and lower, his hard cock was protruding.

I wanted it in my mouth.

I lay on my back. "I'm going to spin around. Get on your hands and knees above me." After a bit of effort, I had my head in the middle of the bed, my feet near the pillows.

Patrick swung his leg over me and shuffled down until his cock was near my mouth. I used one hand to stroke it before sucking it past my lips, his balls resting on the bridge of my nose—his belly pressed hard on my chest. Patrick groaned and pumped into my mouth.

The taste of bath oil was strange and tart on my tongue. His scent was still strong through the aroma of it. I knew his nipples were leaking, leaving droplets on my belly containing our pup.

Behind me, I heard Declan enter the room.

Patrick adjusted the position of his hands, spread his legs wider, and stroked my throat with his cock. The angle always made me choke. The bed dipped above my head.

Declan's knees came into view to either side of my ears.

Looking up, I could see Declan's hard cock approaching Patrick's hole. Patrick's cock pulsed in my mouth as Declan slid into him. Patrick's pumping turned to undulating, seeking pleasure from both of us. I reached behind my head and used my hands to hold Patrick's ass open further.

Each time Declan thrust, Patrick's cock was shoved further down my throat. I choked and coughed but I was loving it. I loved my mouth being full of him.

Declan's hands covered mine. His thrusting was gentle, knowing there was an element of mating that was uncomfortable for Patrick. I shut my eyes and whined as Patrick took my cock into his mouth. He bobbed up and down, faster, and faster until I couldn't contain my climax.

I jammed my hips up and filled Patrick's throat.

His cock pulsed in my mouth each time I released my seed.

Declan slapped Patrick's ass. Patrick drilled into my mouth harder, then tensed. His familiar flavor flooded my throat. I knew his shoulders must be killing him. I squirmed out from beneath him. He lowered his chest as best as he could to the bedding, bracing himself.

I moved behind Declan, stroked his shoulders, and kissed the back of his neck. One hand on his shoulder, I used the other to travel down his spine.

On the next withdrawal from Patrick's hole, I slipped a finger down between Declan's ass cheeks. The next thrust caught my hand. During the following unclenching, I found his tight ring with the tip of my finger. His hole was wet. I pressed my finger inside him.

Declan jerked and thrust, trembling, his hole tightening around my finger. A low growl, then a howl. I removed my finger as his thrusting escalated, slowed, then stilled.

He backed up and Patrick rolled onto his side.

I came out from behind Declan. I didn't like the look on Patrick's face. His features were screwed up; brows dipped; eyes closed—thin lips. I knew what was happening when he groaned and grabbed his belly. The mating had encouraged contractions.

I scrambled across the bed to him.

"Do you want me to call anyone?" I asked Patrick.

He shook his head. "I only want you and Declan."

"Okay." It was his choice who he wanted around him. If Patrick ran into trouble, I would call the healer. He lived in the next house over. He could be here in minutes.

Declan arranged himself so Patrick could put his head in his lap.

My Alpha looked up at me.

"Just keep him calm if you can," I said to Declan. "Remind him to breathe."

Declan released a long exhalation, then started stroking Patrick's hair and whispering words of love to him. I put a pillow between Patrick's knees, opening his legs slightly.

"You're going to feel some pressure," I said and caressed two fingers into Patrick's hole. I really had to push but soon found his cervix. It was dilated. This wasn't false labor.

I ran and got the stack of towels that Patrick had put in the guest room.

We spent the next hour reassuring Patrick he was going to be all right. That the pup would be coming soon. Telling him how amazing it was going to be holding the new life.

Patrick's groaning sounds were soon joined by panting and he kept lifting his knee and looking down the length of his body. It was time to push. I positioned myself.

"Push when you're ready," I said as I grabbed a towel. Patrick whined, his body tensed, and his hole widened. It only took two more contractions and the pup slipped free of his body.

I wiped and rubbed its little body until it started to make squeaking noises. It was a beautiful sound. I teared up. His scent marker was immediately evident. Alpha male like his sire.

We had a new pup.

I brought it to Patrick. He sniffed the pup's silky, black head but was too tired to take him from me. I set the pup at a teat and encouraged him to latch on. He made sweet happy noises as he sucked and started to feed. I leaned in and kissed Patrick on the head.

His eyes fluttered open.

"His name is Taylor," he said.

I sucked in a breath, overwhelmed. There was no stopping the tears that spilled and coated my cheeks. I looked at Declan who nodded and smiled. I turned back to Patrick.

He was my perfect mate.

"I love you," I said to him.

"Love you too," Patrick whispered to me as Declan stroked his hair, and then he closed his eyes. We were committed to one another. The three of us formed an unbreakable bond.

But I knew.

What Patrick and I had was special beyond all of that.

He was mine.

And I was his.

For all eternity.

Epilogue

It really wasn't necessary, but Harlan and Logan had put together a shower for us to introduce our pups to the East Creekside pack. Rose, Harry, Haley, and Reese were beyond excited. And Bryant, Greyson, and Hunter's two sets of twins were more than a little curious. They wanted to hold our two young pups. We weren't ready to let anyone hold them yet.

Except Adam—because he was a professional pup holder.

Lucas was content to look on.

Little Taylor yawned in Patrick's arms after his latest feed. He was growing fast. At 4 weeks old, he was becoming more mobile when we set him down on a blanket, stumbling around as he searched for his next meal. He was going to be a big wolf like his sire.

Mark and Reese looked down at my little bundle of grey fur. I'd named her Patricia. Jonas and Damon had teased us about our choice of names. Taylor and Patricia. No one truly understood what those names meant to us. No one truly understood how much Patrick and I loved each other.

Even Declan didn't fathom the depth of our devotion to one another.

But he encouraged it. Loved to see us in love.

We had so many incredible days ahead of us.

Raising our pups together.

There could be no greater gift.

God, I love him.

About the Author

JT Fader is an alternate pen name for Leigh Jarrett (she/he), allowing Leigh to explore their love of MM+ paranormal and fantasy stories by creating their own worlds.

In their hometown of Victoria, BC, Canada, Leigh can be found nestled up with their fabulously supportive wife and trusty laptop or enjoying the wondrous Vancouver Island outdoors.

To stay up to date with JT Fader's new releases and promos, check out their JT Fader Fantasticals website at www.jtfader.com.

You can also find Leigh on Bluesky.